Cowboy on the Wrong Train

Mouse with a Clue

Jeanne Ann Off

Published in the United States of America

ISBN 978-1-958518-29-8 (SC)
ISBN 978-1-958518-31-1 (HC)
ISBN 978-1-958518-30-4 (Ebook)

Jeanne Ann Off Publishing
10495 E 120th Ave.
Henderson. CO. 80640-9742
http://jeanneanneoffbooks.com/

Order Information and Rights Permission:

Quantity sales. Special discounts might be available on quantity purchases by corporations, associations, and others. For details, contact the publisher at the address above.

For Book Rights Adaptation and other Rights Permission. Call us at toll-free 1-888-945-8513 or send us an email at admin@stellarliterary.com.

TABLE OF CONTENTS

PART I

Chapter 1

Tyler Grenshaw watched Banshee glare at the imposter, then warn Scooter with a hiss that he wasn't welcome to feast on her food or even approach the pan of dry cat food. The two domestic short hair cats stared at each other with arched backs and inflated tails, and a strong desire to avoid actual claw contact. Ty's cat must put the stranger in his proper place without personal injury. Banshee hissed again just before Ty's cell phone rang he Grenshaw home. Scooter ran off to his own pan of food while Ty answered the phone.

"I'm back," said Patti Dileo.

Scooter came slinking back noiselessly, somehow knowing the lady he owned was talking inside the de vice held in Ty's hand. Banshee sat near Ty giving her pretty calico fur a bath. The yellow haired butterfly tab by, Scooter, kept his distance from Banshee.

"I've got an earlier flight on a private plane bringing four men to Gully. I overheard the man who rented the six seat single engine Piper Meridian say he wanted to buy some land. It might be an opportunity for Gully Real Estate to make a sale. Can you pick me up?"

"I'll be there in 35 minutes." Ty knew he could shower in eight minutes and drive from the cattle ranch where he had lived all his 18 years, to the town of Gully wearing clean clothes to pick up his girlfriend at the airport. He hesitated when the phone rang again. Should he answer it? The call shouldn't take long. He answered his cell phone. Scooter sharpened his claws on a piece of driftwood kept for Banshee's nail care. "Ty, its George here. Would you do me a big favor? Meet me at ten Wednesday night at the back of Old Historic Church. I think it is important. Park out of sight and be quiet. Go inside the back door without being seen. Don't ever go on the north side of the building! The neighbor's dog barks. The south side will be safe. Do be on time. That's important. The back door will be unlocked, but the lights will be off. I'll explain after you're inside." "I need my sleep before going to work at dawn. How long will this take?" "Oh, maybe a half hour or so. It is supposed to happen at 10:15 sharp, I heard. There won't be any boring church service. It might get exciting. You'd be a witness. Come on. You'll be glad you came."

"Knowing you and the time and that no services are held there anyway, I wouldn't expect a church service. Half-hour should be okay. I'll be there. Got to go."

"See you tomorrow night."

Ty looked at his watch. The call only took a couple of minutes. He should get to the airport about the same time as the plane from Wyoming.

As Ty went toward the bathroom for his shower, his mother called to him, "Ty, please help me open this jar. The lit in too tight for me.

Ty dutifully went to the kitchen. The lid was too hard to get off by just turning it. Ty put the metal lid under hot water running from the faucet for about two minutes. Then he used his mother's jar opener and the lid came right off. I'm going to pick up Patti at the airport."

"Has she gone to Wyoming to visit her parents?"

"Yes, but she has to be back at work tomorrow morning."

3

Then you'll go to the airport three hours from now.

"No, she is riding in a private plane instead of taking the commercial flight. I want to be at the airport when the plane lands."

Why a private plane? Commercial jets are safer."

"She might get a real estate sale by riding with someone who wants to buy. would like to wash off the dirt and sweat I got from working cattle today"

Were you vaccinating heifers?"

"Yes"

Next cattle working day I suppose you'll gather the steers sold on the video auction and wean them onto trucks.

"Right"

The conversation with his mother was difficult to end. As Ty hurried to his room for clean clothes, he saw that time for his eight-minute shower was gone. Instead he ran out to his old pickup. A cloud of dust followed the speeding green pickup on the gravel road from the cattle ranch. Mother works for Cal too, feeding him and his hired help, Ty was thinking as he drove. She needs to get supper ready. I have worked for Cal since I became of legal age to have a job. Dad is Cal's maintenance man. Even my brother and sister work for Cal when Saturday is a cattle working day. Patti knows all this. She understands I get dirty working. She grew up on a ranch too. She'll understand. Never the less, Ty wished he'd showered, even though that would make him late.

When he arrived at the small airport, the plane had not only landed, but was leaving with two men Ty wanted to put his arms around Patti and kiss his girlfriend, but he knew he was dirty, wore jeans with patches a torn blue plaid shirt and plain brown riding boots which had never been polished. Too late he knew he should have allowed more than 35 minutes even though Patti would have to wait for him in the hangar where she was waiting for him now.

Patti asked, "How's Scooter?"

"He's fine."

"Did you bring him with you?"

"No, he's at the ranch. Do you want to get a bite to eat at the Saddle Sore before we go to the ranch to get your cat? Scooter is okay. He and my cat sorted things out while you visited your parents."

"Sure. It will give us more time together." Patti smiled at Ty and took his left hand while his right handled her small rolling suitcase. Ty loved the feeling of electricity and excitement the touch of Patti's hand gave him.

"Do you know the two men who left to return the plane?" Patti asked.

"No, at least not from the glimpse I got." Ty said.

"There were four men on the private plane. They called each other Skeet, Benton, Rodney and Dieter Dieter is the pilot. Rodney, the youngest one, left with Dieter. Benton is older than Skeet who is older than Dieter

"You talked about possibly selling some land to the man who rented the plane, What sort of land? Does Gully Real Estate have the kind he wants listed for sale?"

"That was Skeet. He talked about buying a small ranch. Dieter and Rodney talked about renting a helicopter and Dieter flying that to Colorado. Apparently Skeet wants to look at ranch land from the sky first He talked like he had lots of money."

It takes a lot of money to buy a ranch these days, even a small one."

Ty wished he didn't have to let go of Patti's warm hand when they got into the dilapidated pickup. The Saddle Sore Inn was crowded, partly because the food was tasty and partly because there were only two restaurants in the small town of Gully. Ty and Patti slipped into a booth.

Patti had a clear view of the parking lot. Ty watched her brown eyes follow a slender young man taller than five foot ten inches with his striking mop of towhead blonde hair and neat clean western clothes as he walked from his new Dodge Ram pickup into the restaurant. Ty knew Patti had dated

Sonny Calhoun before he went out with him. He felt a ferocious twinge of jealousy and sat up straighter. Two men walked in after Sonny One came in a red Hyundai and the other in a white four-wheel drive Jeep Wrangler.

Ty gazed at Pat She was looking in Sonny Calhoun's direction as he sat in a secluded booth with the two men. He thought of his dishwater blonde hair, comparing it with the striking towhead blonde of Sonny's hair. His quite disposition wasn't as popular in high school as the outgoing Sonny. He wasn't as good at basketball as he sax foot four inch tall Sonny.

Patti shook him from his pity party. "Those two men with Sonny are Skeet and Benton."

Ty ashamedly realized it was Skeet she was looking at and perhaps wondering, as he was, why the implement dealer's son was with a man who wanted to buy a small ranch. Probably Skeet had talked about buying equipment. He'd need that for the ranch.

A lanky water wearing western boots with walking heels, new blue jeans and a red western shirt with silhouetted horses galloping across it asked what they would like to drink.

Ty took his eyes off Patti long enough to answer, "Lemonade."

Green ice tea, no sugar said Patti

Here in the restaurant, Ty was especially conscious of his sweat stained Stetson hat and dirty work clothes. He took off the hat. A shower and clean dress clothes would have made him feel less conspicuous if Pas had come on the later scheduled flight.

Now Patti was looking at her menu. Ty did likewise and the waiter came back with their drinks, he ordered his favorite, a porterhouse steak with a baked potato. Patti ordered a chicken salad.

"Skeet doesn't look like a rancher," the thin muscular Ty remarked. "He is somewhat on the plump side Benton looks more like a gray haired old farmer in his coveralls."

"On the plane they talked about investments in the stock market, gold and platinum. The current economy was the main theme. Low interest rates on mortgages seem to have attracted Skeet to real estate. He is wearing a business suit such as an eastern city dweller might wear to an office. Ranches we have listed cost from a million to ten million dollars. Buyers usually are buying as an investment and hire someone knowledgeable to run the ranch until it is sold for a higher price. Ranches such as the Grayson Ranch where you live have been in the family for generations, never coming up for sale. It's too bad Cal Grayson doesn't have any children to pass his ranch on. Do you know why he never married?"

"No, I don't."

"Just t running cattle, sheep or horses isn't enough to pay for a ranch. Some guest ranches that also have cattle and horses do make a profit."

"Skeet could be an investor. A profit in buying a ranch and selling it for a higher price for hunting, fishing and recreation does make the investor a profit."

Ty admired Patti's freckles, rust colored hair, stature almost as tall as his, western clothing including boots pointed for getting into stirrups quickly and high sloping heels. Patti dressed the way he wanted a girl to look. Her friendly brown eyes sparkled when she looked at him. Their food came and they began to eat.

Suddenly a loud argument ensued in the booth where Skeet, Benton and Sonny sat together. Then Sonny was lying on the floor bleeding from the mouth. A commotion from people rushing to help him blocked Ty's view temporarily. When Ty could see Sonny again, Skeet and Benton were gone. So was the red Hyundai with the scrape on one side and a Maryland license plate.

"Stand back!" the doctor ordered as he used chest compressions in hopes of reviving Sonny. The doctor had been in the restaurant to eat supper with his wife and children.

Henri Riddel from the police department along with his partner and a reporter from Kracken de News arrived. The policemen didn't allow anyone to leave and began questioning patrons and Patti told them the Maryland license plate numbers on the red Hyundai that had gone with Skeet and Benton along with their first names, explaining that she had flown to Gully with them. "I also saw a white jeep Wrangler with Maryland license plate. Sonny Calhoun was driving that blue pickup you see parked in front." It also had a Maryland license plate. "Sonny was a student in a university in Maryland. In late spring he came home to his parents who own the Gully Implement Company. After graduating from high school in Wyoming, I came to Gully to work for the real estate company here. I look for out of state license plates in hopes of making a sale

Did you know Sonny?

I dated him a few times, but I didn't like his smoking. He didn't like my cat."

"You say the men he was with came from Wyoming. Where are they now?"

"They left before you came"

Why did they hurry out?

I don't know, Skeet was arguing with Sonny before he landed on the floor. I saw Skeet hit him in the jaw. That probably made him bleed. Is he going to be alright?"

The doctor is working on him. What else do you know?

Skeet came here to buy a ranch. Apparently he wants to look at ranches from the air before going to the land. There are plans to rent a helicopter when the plane is returned."

Finish your meal. We may want to talk to you later," Henri Ridell said.

When Ty and Patti were finally allowed to leave, Sonny had been loaded into an ambulance and taken to the hospital in the neighboring town of Shale.

8

Ty drove past Old Historic Church looking for a good place to park, Several buildings south of the church, he parked along the street.

Would you like to come with me tomorrow night when my friend George wants me to meet him here at ten P.M.? Ty asked

Sure Anytime I can be with you, I'd like your company.

Ty and Patti walked hand in hand to the church, watching out for portions of the sidewalk raised by tree room. Then they walked around the church looking at the beautiful stained glass windows. On the north side a large German Shepherd dog growled, then barked at them. On the south side an office building occupied the space that used to be the parking lot for carriages pulled by horses.

As they walked back to the pickup, Patti commented, "I like the gables with three shades of green scalloped tiles on that old house. There are several with that old style in Gully."

Ty smiled at her. "I do too." Ty stopped in the darkness under a large tree. He remembered his sweaty body then. Standing a little bit away, he asked, "What do you think happened to Sonny Calhoun?"

"Either the stiff upper cut Skeet delivered to his jaw knocked him out, or..." Her voice trailed off.

"Sonny must have gotten involved with Skeet in Maryland," Ty said. "Let's go get Scooter. I have to get up early for work. "George told me to be quiet and unseen tomorrow night. He said he'd explain after I'm inside the back door."

"Sounds mysterious"

"I'll pick you up at 9:45 tomorrow evening. Be ready."

Later at home the radio informed Ty that Sonny was dead.

Chapter 2

Ty stepped lightly onto Cal's 18 year old black and white paint gelding, Cowman, at dawn the next morning. He liked riding the well trained and cared for horse. He took a deep breath of the cool fall air as he rode to the ship per pasture where he would check the cows to be sold, their feed, fence, salt trough and spring water.

A stretch of barbed wire fence was down. Rub marks on wooden fence posts indicated horns had knocked the staples out of those posts. Since none of these cows had horns, he suspected elk. Ty repaired the fence using fence pliers, a fence stretcher, staples and wire he carried on his saddle. As he worked, Cowman grazed and Ty hummed a tune while he thought about Sonny's unconsciousness. He saw tracks of both cows and elk in the soft dirt of molehills. When the fence fixing was finished, he opened the gate to the neighboring pasture and rode on the neighbor's land to look for the AWOL cows.

Cowman was directed toward the old Calhoun homestead, Sonny's great-grandparents place. The cows probably went this way because the grass is better, but it is nostalgic for me because of last night, he thought. Although the Calhoun homestead was part of the neighboring ranch, Ty knew both neighbors were welcome to hunt for any livestock that weren't where they should be.

The nice fall day was crisp and invigorating. Migrating birds ate currents, serviceberries and wild raspberries that grew on bushes beside the old wagon trail Ty rode along. He didn't see tracks from the missing cows, but they were likely to be in grassy areas instead of on the road. He kept watching for tracks and especially for movement off the road. The road veered away from the fence, down a sagebrush-covered hillside, then through Quaking Aspen and Pinion Pine trees. A rocky outcrop had a lot of berry bushes around it. Below was an old mine shaft. At the bottom of the hill a small stream flowed through a tangle of pussy willow trees that had soft pussy's every spring.

Before crossing the stream Ty saw movement in the willows. A closer look revealed one of Cal Grayson's cows with her newborn calf that she was licking dry. Ty knew Cal would not be happy about the unexpected calf born so late in the year. The bulls Cal owned were kept far away from his cows after breeding season, so this would never happen. Markings on the calf revealed she didn't come from any of Cal's Angus bulls. These were Pinzgauer markings, the white strip from the tail-head along the part of the back nearest the tail of the black calf born to an Angus cow. Nobody Ty could think of had a Pinzgauer bull.

The calf was healthy, so Ty left the pair alone for now. It should be an hour or two before move them, he thought.

Ty drank spring water from his canteen as he continued riding toward the Calhoun homestead. Three more of his boss cows were found grazing closer to the homestead. Ty rode past them looking for others, but not finding any. At the top of a large hill he saw the ramshackle log cabin and small barn that were the Calhoun homestead. As he came closer, he saw the corral fence had been repaired since he'd last been there. The road down the hill took him out of sight of the buildings, and then he was beside them suddenly.

There were lots of unexpected tire tracks, all since the recent rain. Duncan Meter, who managed this ranch for investor owner Bret Holden, used this part of the ranch for pasture and hunting. Maybe hunters would use the cabin and put their horses in the corral, he thought.

A crash inside the barn startled Ty. He tied his horse out of sight and walked to the barn window. Mud under his boots didn't phase him. Inside he saw a well-bedded stall with a Pinzgauer bull inside. The man he recognized as Benton was giving the bull hay from an overturned wheelbarrow.

Ty thought. About news of a bull stolen from a show in Canada several months ago. Could this be the bull? Recently four horses were stolen, one being Old Dolly, his boss elderly mare that Cal planned to take to the auction when he went there to watch his cattle sell. Suspecting he'd better not reveal himself to Benton, Ty went to his horse and rode to the three grazing cows. It was easy to drive them to the cow with the newborn calf that was standing and nursing when he got there. Ty let the other cows graze until the calf was two hours old, eating his sack lunch while he waited.

When he began to move the cattle toward their home pasture, going slowly and letting the calf rest frequently wasn't enough even though she was a strong healthy baby. They were resting away from the road when Ty heard the sound of a car engine. The white Jeep Wrangler was traveling on the old wagon road toward the Calhoun homestead. Ty didn't recognize the driver. He was young, fat and kept his eyes on the bumpy trail as he drove slowly. Ty knew the road to the homestead from the ranch headquarters had good gravel, but this ordinarily unused portion wasn't graveled at all. The Jeep was wallowing in mud and moving slowly as its four-wheel drive made the ruts deeper. Ty took his cell phone, only to discover there was no service here. The cell phone tower wasn't within view. He felt a sense of urgency.

Riding slowly up to the baby heifer, letting her become accustomed to his horse standing beside her, then dismounting, Ty grabbed her leg. She tried to get away. Her mother became upset. Expecting this, Ty had his horse between himself and the cow. He was above the horse on the hillside, so picking the calf up and lifting her onto his saddle wasn't too difficult for him. Ty got on behind the cantle and calf. The anxious mother cow followed closely as he drove the other three to the gate. Ty dismounted to open the gate, remounting and herded the cattle into their own pasture before he expertly lowered the calf to the ground. While the calf ran to her mother, Ty shut the gate.

He drove the cattle out of sight of the fence, then galloped into a clearing, where the cell phone worked "Gully Police Department, "a girl answered.

"I just saw the white Jeep used by one of the men who sat in the booth with Sonny Calhoun the night he died, but he wasn't driving. It was on an almost unused road that led to Sonny's grandfather's homestead and driven by a younger man."

"Who is this?"

"Ty Grenshaw."

"Why were you there?"

"To take some cattle home that got into the neighbors pasture."

"Did you get a good look at the driver?"

"He was young and fat, had white skin and wore a dark blue jacket."

"Did you know him?"

"No. He was a stranger to me."

"Where is this almost unused road?"

"On the ranch Duncan Meter runs. Do you know where that is?"

"Wait. I will give the phone to a man who should."

Ty didn't have to wait long.

"Hello. Where did you see the Jeep?"

"East of the Calhoun homestead on the ranch Duncan Meter operates."

"I know where his headquarters are and will send someone out there now. Thank you for calling."

It was late afternoon and Ty had chores to do before he was off work for the day. He galloped Cowman where it wasn't too steep, then walked the last mile to headquarters. This helped cool off the horse and prevented any tendency toward becoming barn-sour. Before starting his chores, Ty turned

13

the unsaddled horse out to pasture and walked to Cal Grason, who had just driven into the yard.

"You have a newborn calf."

"What!"

"One of the cull cows gave birth to a heifer today." Cal frowned.

"Who might own a Pinzgauer bull? The calf has Pinzgauer markings."

"Nobody, as far as I know. A calf would be a nuisance this fall. You feed the calf milk replacer morning and evening after I ship the culls. If you take care of this calf, she is yours. Get a brand and put your brand on her."

Ty was surprised that Cal would give him the unwanted calf. He thought the cow and calf would be sold at auction as a pair.

The sound of a helicopter caught their attention. Ty saw that it was red. Kyle and Dedra, Ty's younger brother and sister, came out of the house to watch the helicopter. Ty's cat Banshee ran under the porch to hide. Hadn't Patti mentioned that Dieter and Rodney were going to return the rented plane and rent a helicopter? Was this the helicopter?

Chapter 3

The cell phone rang a tune on Ty's belt, a call from Patti. "The newest employee at Gully Real Estate just called me with a strange message. Marci must have needed to talk to someone and called me. Now I'm calling you for that same reason. Marci said she and her husband Duane were supposed to carpool to a get acquainted sup per that Resurrection Fellowship in Shale has for newcomers to that church. A red car did come and Duane got in, but the car sped away before Marci could get inside. She remembered that the car had a Maryland license plate. We saw a red car with a Maryland license plate outside the Saddle Sore when Sonny was killed. What do you think?"

"Was it Skeet or Benton that came to the restaurant driving a red Hyundai with a Maryland license plate?"

"Skeet."

"Could Marci be talking about the same car? Did she describe the driver?"

"No. I'll ask her if she can. She said she made other phone calls before she called me. First to her mother who quoted a Bible verse to her."

"A Bible verse? What for?"

"Something I didn't understand about casting her care on God."

"Was her other call to 911?"

"Not then, she called Marshall's. The landline was dead and there was no answer at either cell phone. Then she called the babysitter caring for her children and they were fine. I told her to call 911.She sounded very upset."
"A helicopter we were watching just flew out of sight. Weren't Dieter and Rodney planning to rent a helicopter?"

"Yes. I'm surprised you remembered those names."

"Dieter is an unusual name and I recalled Rodney's when I saw him earlier today driving the white Jeep that was parked outside the Saddle Sore."

"Where did you see him? I thought you had ranch work to do today."

"I was doing ranch work," Ty said defensively.

"Rodney drove to the ranch?"

"Not where I live. He was on the ranch Duncan Meter's runs next to ours. The Jeep was on a muddy old wagon trail leading to the Calhoun homestead. I was driving some of my boss cows home that weren't supposed to be there."

"Oh, I'm sorry I questioned you."

"That's okay, I guess.

"What was the helicopter doing? Your ranch isn't for sale and the one next to you isn't either. I told Dieter where to look and those ranches aren't anywhere near yours. The smallest one is closer to Shale and | also said for them to look at a better ranch south of yours. They said they would look at both, but didn't want to look at the very expensive one east of Gully. We only have three listed."

"Well, that red helicopter was just flying overhead. If one ranch was closer to Shale north of us and the other one for sale is south of us, they could have been flying from one to the other when they went over us here."

"Of-course. I'll see you later when you pick me up for the Old Historic Church caper."

"Nine forty-five sharp. Be ready."

"I'll be ready to go. Bye."

"Bye."

Ty went to the machine shed where his dad repaired some equipment. As Ty worked he wondered if there was any connection between the conversation George told him he heard in Mike's Bar and the men planning to buy a small ranch and Marci's distress.

Ty finished a welding job and went to eat one of his mother's delicious suppers. At 9:00 P.M. he started his old pickup and drove to Gully. He hadn't explained why he was going out so late. He arrived at Patti's apartment building 9:27 P.M. Even though he was early, Ty went up the stairs and rang the bell beside her door.

"Ty. I'm ready. See, a girl can be on time."

"You're special. I even showered and put on clean clothes this time."

"I know you would have day before yesterday too if I'd come on the commercial flight. I understood."

"That's a relief!"

"Let's go to the church and park nearby, so we will be at the back door at ten."

"Sure."

Ty parked two blocks from the church and they walked silently to the back door of Old Historic Church. Ty thought of the usual events at this church: wedding and baby showers, weddings and wedding receptions, but not church services. The Gully parks and recreation department rented the building for those events. Did George somehow get a key from the city?

Just before ten Ty and Patti went inside through the unlocked back door. It was dark and unfamiliar. Ty pondered his uncomfortable feelings and held Patti's hand tighter. A step forward created an eerie creak. Something moved fast nearby. Maybe a mouse, Ty hoped Patti was quiet beside him, her warm hand still in his. The floor creaked again as they stood still in the dark.

George whispered, "You did come. Is that Patti with you?"

How George knew in the dark, Ty wasn't sure. "It is very dark in here," he whispered.

"The streetlight lets me see a little when l face the door. He should be here at 10:30 to get the lock box that is under the front steps. Watch out the window in front near the door. I'll lock the back door. The front is already locked. I have the key I found on a nail under the front steps. There is a lock box under the front steps that a man should pick up."

"Who are we watching for?"

"I don't know. Just get a really good look at him so you can recognize him again. I will watch out the other window. Let's get in position now."

Still wondering why this mattered, Ty with Patti in hand followed George and his small flashlight. George left Ty and Patti beside the small window to the right of the front door, then continued to the window left of the door. Ty saw the flashlight beam go out. They waited, standing in silence and stillness.

It seemed like forever to Ty as he waited. He was tired and sleepy when he saw a large young man walk to the front steps, look in all directions then bend down to retrieve the lock box from under those stairs and leave in another direction. Patti whispered, "It's Rodney."

Because of the streetlight Ty could see Rodney was Caucasian with tattoos on most of his visible skin, large round black earrings in both ears, had a small gold nose ring in his flat nose, dark brown hair worn in a mid length pony tail, round swarthy face, eyes close together, crooked fingers on hands that looked

18

rough and dirty, a chubby person who walked with a slight limp, was about 5'10"and 18 to 20 years old. Rodney walked away with the lock box.

Before moving Ty saw a truck pulling a gooseneck trailer come up the street, stop and admit Rodney into the back passenger seat on the right side. Before the truck moved away Ty heard a bull beller. He couldn't see the truck license plate, but memorized the trailer plate. The bull bawled again.

George was beside them then and said, "Quick! Let's follow that truck.

"Without thinking, Ty and Patti ran to and jumped into George's car a block away and sped after the truck and trailer going toward Shale.

"How did you know about this drop?" Ty asked.

"The evening Sonny Calhoun died I was in Mike's Bar with Sid. I was going to the back room to see if there was a game of poker when I overheard about this drop. I told Sid I'd better get home."

"If you didn't ask Sid to be a witness, why?"

"He gets drunk and talks too much. You don't get drunk or go to Mike's Bar."

"I like my job. Drinking would interfere with that."

The paved road was narrow with many curves for fifteen miles. Ty was glad George slowed when he caught up with the truck and trailer. A half-mile before reaching Shale, the truck and trailer turned right onto a dirt road.

"Don't follow them up that road!" Ty said.

George stopped on a wide place next to the mailbox by the dirt road. "Why not?"

"That road dead ends at Frank Courtler's ranch. He is an old man who is probably asleep now."

Patti broke her silence. "The meadow and barn were listed for lease and the hay for sale. I will find out tomorrow if anyone leased those and if so who. We already know Rodney is in that truck. He was on the chartered plane I flew on from Wyoming the same day Sonny Calhoun died. Tomorrow I show the Fenner Place to Skeet who wants to buy a small ranch. Skeet was on that plane with Rodney and two other men. Ty and | both have to get to work tomorrow morning. It's late. Let's go home."

Ty smiled. "She's right. George, you and Sid need jobs."

"Aw, okay. Patti, let me know if someone leased this place." Somewhat reluctantly, George turned the car around and drove back to Gully.

Chapter 4

Banshee crept slowly to the corner of the machine shed; eyes fixed on the tall grass by the wall. Suddenly she pounced with speed and perfect athletic ability. The unsuspecting mouse was firmly grasped in her teeth. Unsurpassable would describe her skill as a killing machine. She was also skillful at avoiding the beautiful golden eagles, coyotes and red tailed hawks that wanted her to become their food instead of being a pretty orange, black and white calico cat. The playful cat made the mouse endure her amusement for a short time before becoming a much-enjoyed meal.

Ty watched his cat, then helped his boss load his pickup with necessities for erecting elk fence around hay stacks. The day ended with Ty very tired because he'd worked hard after inadequate sleep. After supper he dropped into an easy chair and fell asleep without noticing that his calico cat had curled up on his lap. Ty was in bed when a loud knock pounded on his bedroom door after midnight.

"Ty, the sheriff wants to talk to you," his mother said.

The deputy sheriff opened the door and switched on the light. "Wake up!" he said, then shook Ty's shoulder. Then he picked up one of Ty's boots and compared it with a plaster cast he'd taken beside the Calhoun homestead barn. "Get up. I need to ask you a few questions."

Ty rubbed his eyes.

"Get dressed. You need to come with me to Gully."

Ty obeyed, still more than half asleep.

When they reached the building shared by the Gully Police Department and the Vaca County Sheriff's Department they walked inside. "Sit here," the deputy said to Ty. He sat on a chair next to a table in the interrogation room. "Why were you by the window of the Calhoun homestead barn?"

"I was looking at Benton feeding a Pinzgauer bull," Ty said.

"Benton? You knew the man. Why didn't you just go inside the barn?"

"I knew the name, not the man. I thought maybe I'd found a cattle rustler, so I didn't want to be seen. A Pinzgauer bull was stolen from a livestock show in Canada. Cattle rustlers are usually armed and dangerous. I'd just found a Pinzgauer calf born to one of Cal Grayson's cows that day. Cal doesn't have a Pinzgauer bull or know anyone who does."

"Why do you know the name Benton?"

"My girlfriend Patti rode on a plane from Wyoming to Gully with Benton. She and I saw him in a booth with Sonny Calhoun and a man called Skeet the night Sonny died. Benton was wearing the same coveralls in the barn that he was wearing in the Saddle Sore."

"Do you know where Benton and Skeet are now?"

"No, but Patti works for Gully Real Estate. She was to show the Fenner Place to Skeet today."

"Did she?"

"I don't know. Haven't talked to her since work."

"What else can you tell me?"

"Last night I heard a bull bawl in a trailer pulled by the four door pickup I saw Rodney get into. Patti said Rodney was one of four men on the plane, Skeet, Benton, Rodney and Dieter."

"Where were you when you heard the bull?"

"At Old Historic Church."

"What time?"

"About 10:40 P.M."

"Why were you there?"

"My high school classmate George asked me to be there."

"What else do you know?"

"George wanted to follow the trailer, so we followed it to the Frank Courtler ranch road just before we got to Shale. I didn't want to follow it any further."

"Why not?"

"Work early the next morning plus not wanting to wake up Frank. He's old and leases his meadow and barn and sells his hay. Patti could find out if Gully Real Estate leased those and if so, to whom."

"Okay. We may want to question you again. I'll take you home now."

Chapter 5

"Today I want you to look at the shipper cows and check on your new calf," Cal Grayson said.

Ty eagerly saddled Cowman and rode to the pasture. His newborn calf looked healthy and waged her tail as she nursed. Ty counted the cows twice. Two were missing. The fence was down in a different place. Ty fixed it, then rode into Duncan's pasture. Starting at the east end of the pasture where the wagon trail entered it he looked for the cows. Without finding them before reaching the Calhoun homestead west of the Grayson ranch, he decided to ride uphill instead of down. There would be some grassy openings in the otherwise treed pasture.

Hunters would be in this pasture soon, so Ty was especially eager to be sure no Grayson cattle were in this pasture and were shipped with the other cull cows instead of being mistaken for game. Surely they would be in one of the grassy clearings. They weren't in the first that he came to, so he went higher. Nor were they in the second, so he rode higher. The deer trail he followed became narrow. There was no sign of the cows such as a manure pile. Where could they be, Ty wondered. High above the grazing land he heard a train whistle. Train tracks went through numerous tunnels. Below the tracks the steep hillside was covered with rocks. Those rocks served well to keep cattle, deer and elk off the tracks, but not Rocky Mountain Sheep or mountain goats.

Ty rode closer to the rocky slope. Looking left and right for signs of cattle, he failed to realize that there was no place for a horse to turn around, as the trail became dimmer. When Ty saw the predicament, he went ahead hoping there would be a wide enough place for the horse to reverse directions. Finally coming to such a place, Cowman was as eager to turn around as Ty. He did so, very careful to preserve his life. They descended to a grassy expanse surrounded by Quaking Aspen with yellow leaves. Ty hobbled Cowman and let him graze while he ate his sack lunch. A few fluffy white clouds moved east overhead. Ty heard another train whistle.

Cowman was still grazing. The day was beautiful, peaceful and inviting. It won't take me long to climb up to the tracks, look at the pasture from that high vantage point and perhaps see the cows without spending hours going through trees, he thought. Thinking he would save time, Ty left the horse and walked up to the tracks. As he looked around, sure enough he saw the two missing cows in a clearing just west of the one where Cowman grazed. Then he heard another train coming. It was a passenger train, but not from Amtrak. Maybe it was a special excursion train that stopped beside him as he stood on the rocks below. Curiosity got the better of Ty's usually good judgment when he saw that the steps into the train hadn't been raised. Ty went up those steps and onto the train.

He heard steps approaching, and suddenly the train began moving. Ty looked out. I don't belong here, but if I jump out of this moving train I'll surely break a leg on those slippery rocks. Ty hid behind a curtain covering a baggage closet. He could barely see a man in a conductors uniform, then hear him raise the steps he had foolishly climbed. Next he was listening to the conversation between people approaching.

"Isn't the scenery beautiful?"

"We want it to stay that way. This is the sort of land for Rocky Mountain Sheep, wild goats, bear, wolves, wolverines, elk and deer. They need this habitat. We came here to see the damage we've heard cattle and sheep ranching is doing to wild range-land."

"I've also heard that, but have heard that ranchers rather than overgrazing, take care of the land better than the public does on government land because they won't make money if they destroy the land where they make their livelihood."

"We are here to observe the truth."

"I've heard sheep pull up grass by the roots while they eat. Could that be true of wild sheep such as Rocky Mountain Big Horns here in Colorado and Dall sheep in Alaska or just of domestic breeds?"

"I don't actually know. We will see if the elk here cause aspen trees to die by eating their bark. I've heard they do, but don't believe that. There is much to research. However, The Secret Organization that we are part of wants to end all cattle and sheep ranching so native wild animals like bison and wapiti use the land instead of people. See how rugged and wild this area is? Humans shouldn't populate this land."

"The Secret Organization sent five men here to watch all year around, undercover by having a cattle and sheep ranch. They just arrived here and we are here to help them get started."

"Right! Skeet is the name of the man in charge of the others. Maybe now he has to hire another man because one died."

"The old man who knew the most about livestock?"

"No, the young man who came from Gully was the one that died."

"How?"

"I haven't been told."

"Have you been told why?"

"No."

Ty didn't want to be discovered, but found the conversation interesting. He kept listening. The train moved farther away from Cowman.

"How will The Secret Organization put ranchers out of business?"

"I don't know the details, just that all human use of animals must end. I believe animals are being exploited. I believe animals and humans are equally entitled and that humans are animals."

"Some people teach that there is an all-powerful God who created man in His image with body, soul and a spirit that can know God, but that animals have only a body and soul."

"You don't believe that, do you?"

"No, but there are people who do."

Ty thought about what they were saying. He also thought about the big bang theory he was taught in school. It never made sense to him. He'd seen explosions. Those destroyed rather than making anything but rubble. He thought of primeval ooze. What he supposed was similar at the edge of sloughs didn't result in evolution. Instead quicksand trapped and caused death when an animal got stuck there. Ty had seen the beauty of what he thought must be God's creation of stars, trees, grasses, flowers, mountains, snow, streams, animals and humans. I haven't been to church much, but got the idea that the people who believed an all-powerful God created all the things he saw every day usually went to church.

"Some humans own animals and make decisions about their life and death. The Secret Organization will end this so all animals will be wild and free."

"The Secret Organization is a clever organization. I joined to help do that."

"Population control will be necessary so humans won't destroy nature like they do now."

"Getting control of the food supply will be necessary too."

"The Secret Organization started the vegan diet. We've shown some cancer can be cured or curtailed by a strict vegan diet."

"I've heard that even though they don't have intelligence, emotion and will, plants need protection too. What will we eat if we don't eat plants?

"Let's not go too far. Old growth forests need protection and clear cutting forests must be stopped, but farming for human food is necessary so long as grasslands are not plowed and no-till drills are used."

"As for human population control, is euthanasia of those who are no longer productive and abortion of every unwanted fetus enough?"

"It should be, but restricting family size among large races is also needed to keep humans from overpopulating our mother earth."

"Our televised messages have convinced some people that tofu is a safer food than beef."

"Not everybody though. We have succeeded in bringing prices producers get down, but there are many who still want to eat beef."

"Let's get another drink while the bar is still open during happy hour."

Ty relaxed some when the men speaking moved away. The train had stopped, so he peeked out to see if he could get off of this train. He saw he was on a trestle over a deep chasm. Drunken men would be even more dangerous than those men sober, he thought. Ty looked at his western hat, coat, shirt, jeans and boots. Those men mustn't see me, but how can I stay hidden? As those thoughts crossed his mind, the train lurched forward and entered another tunnel. As soon as they were out of the tunnel, Ty looked again. The train moved slowly. Since there was some space above the tracks before the land rose sharply, maybe he could get off on that side. I wonder if I can walk back to cowman and get the cows home before dark. I must try now. Only the moon and stars will give light after dark and we don't have a full moon yet. Ty left the curtain and was ready to jump off the train when two men grabbed him by the arms.

"Who are you and why are you here?"

Ty swallowed.

"I asked you who you are and why you are on this train," an angry voice said. "Where did you get on this train? Did you get on when we stopped in the town of Mountainside?"

Ty didn't answer. He was dragged helplessly down a hallway and into a compartment. A blindfold was placed over his eyes. Ty struggled, but it was two to one. Then he felt the tightness with which his arms and legs were tied. With his back to the sink, he was tied to the plumbing pipes.

"Make sure he can't open the window if he gets loose."

"This small window doesn't open."

"What will we do with him?"

"In Shale we'll find the answer when we meet up with our employees. Look at his clothes. I've only seen clothes like this in movies showing cowboys."

"They are cowboy clothes alright. I saw some men wearing clothes like these in Mountainside."

Ty heard the door lock after the men left. He couldn't move much as he tried to alleviate his discomfort and loosen his bonds. The plumbing pipes didn't come apart. After a while it became darker. Much later the train stopped and the compartment door opened. A light invaded the space.

"He's still tied up."

Of-course. I do a good job."

"I talked to Rodney in Shale. He said we'd put him with the other hostages."

"Who is Rodney?"

"A man working for The Secret Organization. Skeet hired him."

"This man has ears. We shouldn't let him hear us talk."

"He's heard too much already. He must die."

Chapter 6

Ty squirmed. Fear gripped him, not only for himself, but also for Cowman. With hobbles would the horse be able to escape predators? Sweat dripped from Ty's forehead. His legs and arms felt numb and cold from lack of circulation. Ty could feel his heart thumping. As he tried to struggle, his numb arms and legs felt some welcome pain. Someone came into the compartment and put duct tape over his mouth. Then he heard the compartment door shut and the lock turned again.

Ty struggled more. Somehow he must get loose and off this train. What did they mean by 'other hostages?' he wondered. We saw Rodney pick up something from under the stairs at Old Historic church. I heard the men talk about Skeet. When we followed the trailer carrying the bull to the road into Frank Courtler's ranch, were the 'other hostages' there? Should we have followed them up that road?

Ty's thoughts were interrupted by a lurch of the train.

I'm hungry, was his next thought.

The train was backing. Ty. wondered why.

Then the train stopped and he heard voices as people went past the compartment. The few words he caught were about getting off the train in Shale. Everything became quiet. Nobody opened the door to his compartment. Ty fell asleep. When he woke it was morning, even with the blindfold over his eyes, enough light crept in for him to know it was daylight.

Finally the compartment door opened. Ty shuddered as fear of death gripped him again. His struggles hadn't loosened his bonds. Ty was dragged down the aisle and carried outside and to the place where his feet were untied.

"Walk! We aren't going to carry you any farther."

Where have I heard that voice before? Ty tried to walk, but the tingling in his legs and feet made them feel strange, not taking orders from his brain.

"Move!"

Gradually as the feet and legs resumed normal function, he moved forward with strong hands that directed him in the desired direction.

"Pick up your feet. Walk faster."

Ty did as he was told.

"Help me get him inside."

Ty could feel his left foot elevated to a step. "Push down and lift you right foot!"

Am I being put back on the train? Ty wondered.

Soon he was inside and sitting in a chair. He heard the rotors of a helicopter and then a seatbelt click. He felt it lift off. He still was blindfolded and his mouth duct taped shut. Would he ever see Cowman and the cattle again? Ty had wanted to ride in a helicopter, but not like this. Not much later Ty felt the chopper land. The seatbelt was unfastened and two people got Ty out of the aircraft and led him away. Soon he smelled manure. The sound of his boots on a wooden floor was different from the dirt where they had walked.

"We are already short on food and you've brought another mouth to feed. What are we going to do with these hostages anyway? We don't want to risk asking for ransom money."

"Why do we have hostages?"

"Ask Skeet."

"When will he be here?"

"He went to buy some food. Shortly, I hope. I'm hungry."

"He won't know about the new hostage."

"He sneaked onto the train. I don't know how much he heard, but we can't let him go."

"Tie him to that barn support post. It is solid."

"Rodney, instead of sitting there on a hay bale, clean the bull's stall."

"The bull is in there."

"I'll put him in another stall. He leads very well. After all, he was a prize show bull."

"Where do want me to put the dirty straw?"

"Haven't you seen the pile back of the barn?"

"Okay, okay."

Ty could hear the movement of feet. He assumed they were Rodney's and the other speaker. The sound of a stall door opening and hooves walking on the wooden floor were next." The noises the bull made eating hay and those Rodney made as he pitched wet straw and manure into a wheelbarrow, Ty heard. Then the barn door opened and Ty heard the wheelbarrow was pushed outside. The cold air made Ty shiver. He wished he had the coat he'd tied on his saddle. Someone came in the barn door at the other end. Wind blew through the two open doors making Ty even colder.

"There were three hostages when I left. Now there are four. Three were enough!"

"Why did we even have three?"

Ty heard laughter. "To keep you in line. If you don't do as I say, you will be accused of kidnapping."

"Someone will miss Don and Melanie Marshall and Duane soon enough. There will be people looking for them. We already made a mistake when Duane's wife wasn't taken too. She has probably already caused trouble for us."

34

"Probably so. Don and Melanie Marshall were the only ones I wanted you to grab. Why did you get Duane anyway?"

"We saw his name and address on a list in Marshall's house. Food was cooking. They were expecting him as company. We didn't know he had a wife."

"You just said you made a mistake when you didn't take her too. Your lies catch up with you and are one reason not to ever trust you."

"We ate some before we left Marshall's. I wish we'd eaten more, but Dieter said there wasn't time."

"Well, the new hostage can have the sandwich I bought for you. You are too fat anyway. Ranch work should slim you down. Shut that back barn door. It's cold in here."

Ty rubbed the ropes that tied him against the post he was tied to even though that proved futile. Someone ripped the duct tape off Ty's mouth and untied his hands, then shoved a sandwich in them. Ty ate the fish sandwich eagerly.

A voice he hadn't heard before said, "Thank you for the sandwich."

"Shut up!"

There were sounds of eating, but nobody else spoke until a man's voice said, "Bathroom time."

Ty heard someone walking to the door. Finally it was his turn, but no opportunity for escape occurred. Ty was soon inside the barn and tied to the post again. They forgot to put duct tape over his mouth, but retied his hands behind Ty's back. The door opened briefly as his captors left. No captor spoke and silence remained for several minutes. Then Ty spoke, "I'm Ty Grenshaw from the Cal Grayson ranch. Who are you?" "I'm Don Marshall. I was taken from my own garage in Shale. In the struggle my right arm was broken and a bone protrudes. Every time it moves it hurts a lot and by now the swollen arm hurts all the time. Maybe it has become infected. I probably have a fever, but feel cold. If there hadn't been tape over my mouth, you would have heard me when they took me outside. Whoever took me out wasn't careful and every time my arm was bumped, it hurt more. We were about to have a party and were getting ready for guests, newcomers to Resurrection Fellowship in Shale. Are you familiar with the church?"

"No. I don't go to church," Ty answered.

"I'm Don's wife, Melanie Marshall. I was in the kitchen when suddenly the knife I was going to cut roast beef with, was held at my throat. I was blindfolded and led out, then roughly pushed inside what I suppose was a car. Until now, I didn't know my husband was here or that he has a compound fracture that needs immediate medical treatment. Going outside was very embarrassing for me. It must have been excruciating for him. I haven't seen our kidnappers, have you Don?"

"No, I was blindfolded right after two strong arms grabbed me."

"Have you any hope of getting loose?"

"Not any success so far."

"I was seen and heard I must be killed," Ty said.

"So did you see the kidnappers? Describe them if you can, please."

"The two I heard and saw were the men who grabbed me on the train. I didn't see much before they blindfolded me, but heard plenty. Those people are here to put an end to all animal use by humans. One said he wanted the truth, but it seemed to me his mind was already in favor of ending human use of animals. What l saw of the two was that they were men, one about 6'4" tall and the other about 5'11. Green casual clothes were worn by both. They had black loafers. Neither wore a hat, so I saw brown hair and light brown skin. Their speech was plain English without an accent. Both were very strong."

"I was to be a guest at Marshall's last evening. I saw the man who grabbed me and shoved me into a red Hyundai. He was young, maybe about 18, overweight, smelled of body odor, wore large earrings in both ears, his skin was probably white, but had so many tattoos it was hard to tell. Among the tattoos were snakes, dragons and skulls. His brown hair was in a mid-length

36

ponytail. His eyes were closer together than with most people. He didn't threaten to kill me, but now I'm afraid because that would leave my wife Marci and two children without me while I enjoyed God's heaven. I'm Duane, by the way. I'm not afraid to die because Jesus saved me from my sins penalty. When you said you didn't go to church, okay, no church can forgive sin. Ty, if you are killed and stand before God and He asked, 'Why should I let you into My heaven? 'what would you answer?"

"I'm not sure. I do believe there is a God Who created all the beauty around us and the stars above. I also know I've sinned. I never should have gotten on the train I was kidnapped from, but I did hear the two men talk as if there wasn't any God and that they thought humans were just animals. I don't agree. My boss makes the decisions as to which cattle live and which die on sound principles. Do animals go to heaven?" Ty asked.

"There will be animals in heaven. Horses are mentioned, but I'm not sure they are the same ones we love on earth. In God's millennial kingdom on earth the animals will be vegetarians so the lion and the lamb can lie together without the lion eating the lamb. More on that later, if we get a later. Let's get off this bunny trail and talk about the most important event that can happen to anyone. We can't get to heaven by being good. Most people think good people go to heaven and bad people go to hell. Not so because Romans three starting with verse nine says, 'What then? Are we better than they? No, in no wise, for we have before proved, both Jews and Gentiles, all are under sin. As it is written, There is none righteous, no not one. They have all gone out of the way, they have all become unprofitable, there is none that doeth good, no not one. For all have sinned and come short of the glory of God. 'Ty, you admit you have sinned. Did you know Christ paid your way to heaven on the cross?"

"Uh, I heard that Jesus died on the cross and rose again. Cal and his employees go to church once a year on Easter Sunday. The preacher said Jesus died and rose again and that the tomb was empty. They sang about the resurrection."

"God's justice is real justice. He found man guilty of sin. Man was sentenced to death. No man hasn't sinned, so all humans are sinners, but we sin because we are sinners, we didn't become sinners when we sinned. God has a plan because He loves you and 1 and everyone else. Romans 5:8 says, 'But God commended or proved His love in that Christ died for us while we were yet sinners."

"Christ died for everyone? What about our kidnappers?"

"Romans 6:23 says, 'The wages of sin is death.' Wages are what we earn by what we do. Our kidnappers earned death, but so did I and you too. What did Christ pay? Death. The rest of Romans 6:23 says, 'but the gift of God is eternal life through Jesus Christ our Lord. Heaven is a gift accepted by believing and faith."

The barn door opened and Rodney's spoke. "We forgot to tape their mouths shut." Quickly Ty felt duct tape over his mouth. That must have happened to the other hostages too. None of them spoke and the barn door opening and shutting were the sounds he heard.

Ty mulled over what Duane had said. Just what is believing and faith? He believed Jesus existed, that He died and rose back to life, but didn't quite understand how heaven was a free gift. Come on, I made good grades in school. Why is this hard? Then Ty heard people humming a tune he hadn't heard before, but liked. For at least an hour he listened as the other hostages hummed various tunes.

Except for the music, the day wore on. There was no additional food. Someone did remove the tape and offer water to a very thirsty Ty. After he drank tape was applied again.

Ty counted the days, all four of them. Then he heard the kidnappers talking.

"There are sheriff deputies coming with a search warrant. We must get the hostages out of here. They are sure to search this barn. Let's put them in the trailer and move them off this ranch before the sheriff gets here. Hurry!"

Ty felt his bonds untied from the post he'd sat uncomfortably beside. His legs were freed, but not his hands and he was marched out of the barn. Then his leg was lifted and placed up onto what he supposed was the trailer floor.

38

He smell of manure came to him again. This trailer hasn't been cleaned! When he was rudely set down he felt wet manure underneath.

He was quickly tied to something. Finally he heard the trailer door shut, then the trailer moved forward going fast down a bumpy road. This helped loosen the ties He was already trying to loosen. After several miles of this, at a sharp turn he was thrown out the door that must not have been shut right in the hurry to be gone before the hostages were discovered. Ty felt himself rolling downhill, then land painfully against a tree. He heard a splash, then the bubbling of brook water running over rocks, and a very muffled female shriek.

That must be Melanie and maybe she was the splash I heard. Ty struggled to loosen his the ropes that shackled his feet and get his arms free from the ties holding them behind his back. He rubbed his blindfold against the tree trunk where he stopped. It was cold enough without being in a cold stream. The blindfold slipped down. Ty could see that below him Melanie was in the brook. He calculated. If he could roll down to the next tree below, then to the one below that, could he help Melanie get out? He rolled down to the next tree. Dead branches on the ground poked him. The tree stopped him. He rubbed the ties holding his arms against its trunk. Hurry, he thought as he rubbed. Then he saw Don against another tree in obvious pain. Rolling downhill had further injured his broken arm. Duane was above all of them and hadn't rolled far at all. When Ty looked up at him, he became aware of the roadway just above Duane. Duane was struggling to go uphill and toward the road, bending his knees and inching his way upward.

Ty looked down at Melanie. Don couldn't help his wife or himself. The ties holding his arms wore through and Ty's hands were free. He rolled down to the next tree, paused a moment, then slid down towards the brook feet first. At the edge of the stream he rolled onto his stomach and slid over some smooth rocks until he was close to Melanie. She was turning blue from cold. He reached out and grabbed her clothes. Pulling as hard as he could, she was moved toward him a little. He used his knees to move closer and pulled more, gradually getting her out of the water. He took off his shirt. It wasn't much, but it was dry. He covered her as much as the shirt could. Not sure what to do next, he removed the tape holding her mouth shut then removed the tape from his mouth. She was unconscious. Could he save her life? Ty managed to get his body over hers, hoping to warm her. Don, he called, "Your wife is out of the water and I'm trying to warm her."

The tape was tight over Don's mouth, but he managed a grunt. They Ty heard a car stop above them. Was it someone who would see Duane and help or was it the kidnappers having returned?

Chapter 7

"There is a man below us with his feet and hands tied and tape over his mouth!"

Gloria scrambled down to Duane and Max hurriedly passed them to Ty and Melanie.

"I'm trying to warm Melanie. Have you got a blanket?"

"Here is my coat," Max said as he removed it and put it on Melanie, then carried her to his car.

Gloria released Duane from his bonds, and then both hurried down to Don and Ty, where their bonds were released. Duane helped Don go up to the car while being careful not to touch the swollen arm. Gloria released Ty's feet, put her coat on his bare upper body and led him to the car. The car was crowded with all six inside, Don was in the front passenger seat so his broken arm wouldn't be bumped and Melanie was close between Duane and Gloria with Ty beside Duane. Max drove as fast as he could legally go to the hospital in Shale.

"What happened?" Gloria asked?

"We were held hostage in a stock trailer. The door came open as it went around the corner fast and we were thrown out. I'm so thankful you came!"

"Max and I are here for our younger brother Sonny's funeral tomorrow. We just needed to drive around and think. Rumor says he was murdered. Did any of you know Sonny Calhoun?"

"I did," Ty answered. He was older than I was. My girlfriend and I were in the restaurant when he died."

"You were?" the excited Gloria asked.

Max interrupted. "I think I remember where the hospital is, but can anyone help me get there quickly?"

"Turn left at the next intersection," Don said.

Max was seen driving up to the emergency entrance fast, so emergency personnel met them at the car with a gurney. Melanie was loaded onto the wheeled cart and covered with a warmed blanket, then quickly taken into the hospital. Don walked to the entrance with a doctor. Max moved the car to parking while Gloria accompanied Duane and Ty into the hospital.

Immediately Melanie and Don received medical help. Duane and Ty were asked for insurance information, then checked to see if either had suffered any ill effects. Max and Gloria sat down with Ty when he was found to be okay except for some cuts and bruises, hunger and cold. Duane suffered even less.

"You saw my brother die? Please tell me more," Max said.

Ty told him and Gloria what he had witnessed.

"How did you become hostages?" Gloria asked.

Duane told his story, then Ty his.

When Ty finished, he asked what time and where the funeral would be.

"Two o'clock tomorrow at Gully Bible Church. Dad and Mom own the Gully Implement Store, so they arranged for a service at Gully's only church and interment in the Gully cemetery. All of us are shocked. Our brother had just graduated from college last May."

"Sonny must have been four years older than me. I graduated from high school last May," Ty said.

"Duane, did you know Sonny?" Max asked.

"No, my wife and I just moved here so I could get a job as a lumberman felling trees in the forest and getting the logs to the mill. My wife got a job at Gully Real Estate Company, so she has to drive to Gully to work, but my job is closer to Shale, so we rented a house in Shale. We attend Resurrection

Fellowship in Shale, but even though I didn't know Sonny, I'd like to come to his funeral service, if my boss will give me the time off."

"You are welcome to come, "Max said.

"Where is Gully Bible Church?"

As you enter Gully keep going straight until the first gasoline station. Turn left, go a block and turn right. There is a steeple on the building just ahead on the right."

Ty remembered the cell phone in the pocket of the shirt he'd put on Melanie. When he was examined, he'd been given his shirt and put it on. The phone was still in the pocket. Taking it out, he called home.

"Mom, its Ty."

"Where have you been?"

"Held hostage. I'll tell you all about that when l get home. We are at the Shale hospital now where two other hostages are being treated. I'm okay, but my horse Cowman and the two cows are..."

"The horse and cows are home. Kyle and Dedra brought them when they went to look for you."

"Someone is coming to talk to us. See you as soon as I can."

Chapter 8

"Where were you?" an angry Cal Grayson asked as Ty got out of Max Calhoun's dad's car.

"I'm not sure where we were held hostage, but think it was the Frank Courtler ranch," Ty said.

"Hostage? We? Were you with Patti?"

"No. Don and Melanie Marshall and Duane whose last name 1 don't know."

"This is Don and Melanie who brought you home?"

"No, Max Calhoun and his sister Gloria who came for their brother's funeral tomorrow. They rescued us, took Don and Melanie to the Shale hospital, Duane home, then me."

"Oh yes, now I recognize you Max. I'm so sorry about your loss. Sonny was very young to die. The police say he was murdered."

"We are thankful we went to the right place to make the rescue. Don't be too hard on Ty. He was trying to save Melanie from hypothermia when we found them."

"Mother said Kyle and Dedra brought Cowman and the two missing cows home. Is Cowman okay?" Ty asked.

"Yes, no thanks to you. They found him hobbled and sort of running with his back legs together. There was blood on those back hooves. Perhaps he kicked a coyote. How could you have become a hostage when you were in Duncan's pasture?"

"I hobbled Cowman so I could get high enough to look for the cows from that vantage point instead of riding through the trees without finding them. I did see them eating grass."

"Good, but that doesn't tell me how you became a hostage."

Ty swallowed and looked at the ground. "I shouldn't have become curious when a passenger train that wasn't Amtrak stopped."

"Curious, causing you to do what?"

"I got on the train and heard the enemies of cattle ranching talking. While I listened, the train moved. That train was chartered by some Secret Organization that wants to put ranchers out of business. They caught me and said I must be killed because I overheard them. I was taken to a barn where there were already three hostages. We weren't treated nicely."

"And now that I know you got on the wrong train, can you identify those Secret Organization people?"

"If I heard their voices again, I'd know two of them. I know what Rodney looks like. He held us in the barn. Most of the time I was blindfolded, but Skeet was there and I saw Skeet in the restaurant where Sonny Calhoun died."

"Who is Skeet?"

"The man Patti showed the Fenner Place to and one of the men I heard talk at that barn where we were held. He was in the booth with Sonny and an older man named Benton at the Saddie Sore Inn. I saw hit Sonny in the jaw, dropping him to the floor."

"Did Skeet kill Sonny in front of so many people? I heard the police didn't have a suspect. Kraken de News called Skeet a person of interest."

"I don't know. The blow I saw was enough to knock Sonny out, but for that to kill him doesn't seem likely."

"You will want to call Patti. She has been very concerned about your whereabouts, as we all have. Are you hungry?"

"I sure am! All I've had to eat the last four days is a fish sandwich and some water to drink."

"Come into the house. There is food there," said Ty's mother. She and Ty's dad stood listening, relieved that their son wasn't dead.

"We will be going to our parents now. We got a privilege we didn't expect when we stopped at a wide place by the road. I'm so glad we could help. I'm going to call the hospital to see if they will tell me anything about the Marshall's, "Max said.

"Come inside. I have the phone number in the house," Ty's mother said.

Ty ate eagerly, but didn't stuff himself. His cell phone was still in his shirt pocket. He called Patti at work. "Patti, how are you? Does Marci know her husband is safe?"

"Ty! Where are you?"

"Home. We left Duane at his house, then came here. Duane and I were hostages along with Don and Melanie Marshall. We left that couple at the hospital in Shale. Max Calhoun and his sister Gloria rescued us. They came for Sonny's funeral."

"Duane called Marci and told her. She told me you were with him. Are you okay?"

46

"Mainly I was hungry and thirsty. I just ate. Next I'll shower. Cal said we'd work tomorrow morning, then all six of us ride in his car to Sonny's funeral. We will meet you at Gully Bible Church and save a seat for you if we get there first or you for us if you do."

The next afternoon Gully Bible church was full and there weren't nine seats together, so Ty, Patti, Duane and Marci had four together, while Cal and the rest of Ty's family had five. Soon after they were seated there was standing room only. At the guest book a detective made sure everyone signed in.

Sonny's body was in an open green casket at the front. A man closed it before the service started. The service started with singing by a soloist, then Pastor Malluchi read, "Even though I walk through the valley of the shadow of death, I fear no evil; for Thou art with me, Thy rod and Thy staff, they comfort me." This passage in Psalm 23 isn't about someone who just died; though it's often used at funerals. Instead it refers to a valley in Israel. There is a road, or perhaps we would think of it as a trail, between Jericho and Jerusalem known as 'shadow of death' due to its narrow way and steep sides. King David, who wrote Psalm 23:4, was a shepherd before he was a king. If sheep got on a trail like this one, in the darkness many would slide into the ravine and die. The word shadow implies late in the day when the sun had gone behind the rocks and the dark valley would be treacherous, not only because of the landscape, but because predators would be looking for a meal. David's message is, 'Trust God.' David's confidence is that even if one must walk through this dark valley, he would fear no evil, but walk through with peace because God was with him. The shepherd's rod was a tool used to keep sheep on the narrow road, to keep them from straying off the trail and falling. Psalm 23:4 speaks of the perils of life. Sonny Calhoun faced a peril of life from which he died, even though he was a tall capable young man. Well-trained detectives are looking for the cause of his death.

Many face perils that are not their fault. Job did. Job 3:5 tells us of Job's misery as do Job 12:22; 16:16 and 24:17. In Job 28:22,23 we are told God understands even though Job didn't and God never told Job why. Elihu mentions darkness and shadow of death in Job 34:22 where he tells Job 'There is no darkness, nor shadow of death, where the workers of iniquity may hide themselves.' We hope to find out how our beloved Sonny Calhoun died, but we might not.

Some, like King David, face perils of their own making. Psalm 38 startled me when I read David's words in verses 3-5, 'There is no soundness in my flesh because of Thine anger; neither is there any rest in my bones because of my sin. For mine iniquities are gone over my head: as an heavy burden they are too heavy for me. My wounds stink and are corrupt because of my foolishness.'

I don't know if Sonny's peril was not his fault or if it was because of foolishness.'

You face an eternal peril today if you haven't accepted the fact you are a sinner, believed heaven is a free gift Jesus Christ died on the cross to give you and called on Him to save you, not depending on any good you have done. Romans 10:13 says, "For whosoever shall call upon the name of the Lord shall be saved.' I'd like to talk to you if you have any question about eternal salvation. At this time our soloist will sing."

After the song Pastor Malluchi said, "Sonny Calhoun was a graduate of Gully High School, having attended Gully public schools since kindergarten. He earned a scholarship to the University of Maryland and completed his bachelor's degree there. His death this fall came after working in his parents Gully Implement Store over the summer as he had all through high school and college. He excelled in basketball, earning his letter in that sport in both high school and college. His knowledge of farm and ranch implements was extensive. He was the youngest of three children, two boys and a girl. His parents, brother Max and sister Gloria are here today. We all grieve. At this time I would like those who want to speak to come up front and tell remembrances they have of Sonny."

Max came to the platform. "My younger brother was three inches taller than me. His hair was lighter. He could make more baskets than I could, even though we both played on the high school basketball team. Now I am ashamed of my jealousy. My grief is overwhelming. I want a live brother, the uncle of my two children who are at home with my wife. Those children are so young

48

they won't remember Sonny. We enjoyed skiing in these Colorado mountains, fishing in streams and lakes, and stocking shelves in our parents implement store. More fun than stocking those shelves was driving the tractors in the yard. I don't know what to say about losing my brother other than it shouldn't have happened."

Gloria spoke next. "My brothers were special to me, one older and one younger. Sonny liked to play jokes on me. One time he put a garter snake in my bed. I woke shrieking in the night as I felt that snake crawl over me. Another time | became curious about something he held in his hands. He showed me the spider and I jumped back. He told me the mice he played with had a bite that hurt. The cruelest thing of all is that now he is dead."

Sonny's Aunt spoke. "When Sonny was very young, his parents rented the house they lived in. The landlord came to repair the overflowing toilet. Sonny said to his mother, 'You let that man play in the toilet. Why won't you let me?' The landlord removed the rubber duck that was supposed to be in the bathtub with Sonny."

Snickers rumbled through the room in spite of the solemn occasion. The congregation sang "In the Garden," a hymn about Jesus resurrection.

Pastor Malluchi said, "After the ushers dismiss your row, you can pass the open casket and go back to your seats, then we will go out, pallbearers first, then family, and each row starting at the front, we would like you to line up your cars behind the hearse and family car with your headlights on for the short trip to the Gully Cemetery where services will conclude."

The service at the cemetery was short. The family sat on chairs atop green outdoor carpet while others able to stand stood behind them. Pallbearers placed the casket on the frame that would lower it into the hole below.

Pastor Malluchi opened his Bible and read I Chronicles 22:19a. "Now set your heart and your soul to seek the Lord your God." Next he read from II Chronicles 6:36, "If they sin against thee, (for there is no man which sinneth not), and thou be angry with them, and deliver them over before their enemies, and they carry them away captives,..." He stopped reading without finishing the sentence and looked at the audience, then said, "If Sonny was murdered, his murderer may be arrested or not. Do what you can. That is to obey God by the power only He can give you."

Pastor Malluchi went to each member of the family and hugged them after speaking kindly to each. He turned to those gathered, giving a gesture that the service was over. A man from the Gully Mortuary asked the family to gather at the Calhoun residence so they could grieve together.

Ty noticed that detectives who came to the cemetery whispered to each other and looked in the direction of two men who hadn't attended the church service. Standing with shovel in hand was a man in work clothes standing beside some bushes. The other was wearing a business suit. Ty recognized the man in the business suit as Skeet. He turned to Patti and said, "Skeet is here."

"So is Dieter, said Patti. He's the man holding the shovel."

Chapter 9

"We must do something about that fence between the shipper pasture and Duncan's. It's fine for holding cattle and elk can easily jump over. It's when elk rub on the posts that staples come out. We will have to drive steel posts between each wooden post and wire the fence to those. That is today's job and tomorrow's. Meet you at the pickup in five minutes," Cal said to Ty the day after the funeral.

With the truck loaded with steel posts, slide hammer and wire ties, Cal and Ty worked all day to make the fence tighter. The land was rocky, so driving posts wasn't easy.

Ty was tired, but called Patti after supper. "I'd like to come over this evening."

"I'll be waiting."

"See you in a few."

Patti was waiting for Ty when he arrived. "Skooter would like to go out for his walk. He wears a collar and leash like a dog. I usually take him out for an evening walk. When you came for a date or I have to show real estate, he misses out, but why couldn't we all go together?"

"Would be fine with me. I don't think my cat would ever wear a collar though."

"She has the ranch to roam. Skooter just has this small apartment. Some people let their cats roam around Gully, but the town dog catcher also impounds cats."

"Let's see if there's another drop under the steps at Old Historic Church."

"Okay. Tell me about your adventure while we walk."

"Adventure? I was frightened. They said I must die because I heard them talk on the train."

"That's scary! I meant how you got from the train to being a hostage and then how you got away. Marci told me some she learned from Duane, but we had to work rather than visit with each other. I had papers to prepare for Skeet's closing the purchase of the Fenner Place. I'm interested in both your ordeal and if Skeet is a dangerous man."

Shooter walked ahead of them and went from side to side just as if the cat was a dog. Ty told Patti all he experienced. "As for whether Skeet is dangerous, I don't know, but you should never be alone with him just in case."

They arrived at Old Historic Church. Going to his knees, Ty looked under the front steps. There wasn't a package there, but looking up at the bottom of the steps, he saw a nail with a key on it. "So this might be the key George used to gain entrance. Let's try it."

Ty and Patti went to the back via the south side of the building so the German Shepherd dog north of the building wouldn't be alerted. The key turned in the lock and Ty opened the door. They went inside and closed the door. Ty turned on his flashlight. They walked hand in hand into the sanctuary; past the velvet upholstered pews and to the communion table in front.

Suddenly Skooter dived under the communion table and came out with a mouse in mouth. Patti knelt down and pulled a mouse nest out from under the table. This consisted of scraps of paper and other debris. While Skooter played with his catch and finally ate the hapless mouse, Ty and Patti examined the bits of paper.

"Look at this. It's part of a matchbook cover from the Red Fox. There is a message written on it. 'Meet you at Mike's Bar. Bring' . . . The rest of the sentence is torn off, but the other side has more. 'Secret Organization doesn't trust Nirvana. She goes to the library too...'"

"Who do you suppose Nirvana is?" "Somebody Gully Real Estate had contact with?" "No." "I've heard the word Nirvana somewhere, but don't remember. It might have been in high school, something we studied when the class was about comparative religions." "We had a class like that too. If I remember right, nirvana is the end Hindus or Buddhists desire." "Let's get out of here. Bring that scrap with you." "Okay. I'll put the rest of this mess in a trash container I saw beside the Insurance Company next door. What do you want with the matchbook cover?"

"Secret Organization is mentioned. The train I was on was a Secret Organization train chartered to bring members here to see animal use for themselves. Maybe the Gully Police or Vaca County Sheriff's Department will want that scrap."

"The police and sheriff work together, don't they?" "Yes. They share the same building too." The key was replaced on the nail after locking the door. Patti dumped the mouse nest in the trashcan. "Yes, and we are going to the Police Station now." Scooter seemed glad to get a longer walk than usual.

"We found this scrap and think you might be interested because of The Secret Organization train connection with the kidnapping."

"Where did you get this? It isn't in very good condition."

"It was part of a mouse nest."

"And where was this mouse nest?"

"In Old Historic Church."

"When did you find a mouse nest there?"

"About a half hour ago."

"Why were you there?"

"Walking the cat."

The policeman looked suspiciously down at the cat and his leash. "Weren't you one of the hostages the Sheriff talked to us about? You are Ty Grenshaw, aren't you?"

"Yes." Ty wished he hadn't come. He was tired and realized he was about to be questioned.

53

"Follow me Ty. Leave your friend and the cat on the bench by the entrance."

Ty followed the officer to the interrogation room where he was aware of cameras recording everything."

"Has the Sheriff Department questioned you?"

"Not yet."

"Start at the beginning and tell me everything that happened from start to finish."

Ty started with his ride up the deer trail toward a height where he could look for the missing cows and ended with seeing Skeet and Dieter at Sonny's graveside service. He was surprised Patti and her cat were still waiting when he was finally told he could leave. He wondered about Nirvana as he took Patti and her cat to their apartment and said a quick goodnight.

Chapter 10

"We should finish the fence today. Tomorrow morning we round up everything in the shipper pasture. The trucks load at eight," Cal said.

"What time do we start?" Ty asked.

"Be saddled and ready to ride at 6 A.M."

Patti would ride Cowboy that day, so Ty saddled a young mare, Cowgirl. They were both ready to ride at six. Cal was astride his horse, Ty's dad, mother, brother and sister on more of Cal's horses. The seven of them rode together to the shipper pasture, then spread out to round up the cattle. Most of the riders stayed behind the stragglers while Cal rode ahead to open gates and guide cattle into the corral. Ty's young heifer calf was cut from the herd as soon as the corral gate was shut with cull cows and heifers inside. She was taken to a barn stall with a run out side, where she bawled for the mother she would never see again.

"The semi-trucks arrived just before eight and the first backed up to the loading chute with the door open. Cal tried unsuccessfully to stop eager truck drivers from using electric prods to load the cattle faster. Soon every truck was loaded and on the way to market, an auction 100 miles away. Bred heifers and cows that would calve in May or June would be sold to new owners who wanted to calve them out. Slaughter cattle, cows that weren't pregnant, were lame, or with cancer eye, brisket disease or a bad bag would sell the next day. Two old bulls Cal already had in the corral rode in a separate compartment in one truck.

Younger new bulls would replace them. Bulls that reached five years of age were sold to prevent inbreeding and eliminate either laziness or aggressiveness. Occasionally Cal had to sell a bull that broke his penis and could no longer breed a cow. The two put on a truck today were five years old. Earlier Cal had sold the entire herd of this year's steer calves and smaller heifers by video auction, then had them delivered by truck to their new owners.

Kept at his ranch were good cows and first calf heifers expected to calve within three weeks in April. With today's job done by nine, Cal told Ty and Patti to find out what the sun had caused to gleam in the nearby national forest. After they went through the gate and shut it, they rode along the forest fence.

The glint might be from a rifle, Ty thought, but hunting season didn't start here for several days. Patti was first to see a flash of light in the trees.

"Look over there." "I see it."

They rode toward the flash. Then they saw a thin girl holding a crystal and looking into a mirror.

"Hello. I'm Ty and this is Patti."

The girl looked at them, but said nothing right away. She picked up her coat and snuggled it around herself before she spoke. "Are you from the ranch next to this forest?"

"I am," said Ty. "Are you planning to hunt when the season opens?"

"No. Will there be hunters here?"

"It's likely. There are every year."

"My job is courier for an organization. I took this job not realizing it would be so old at night. I needed a job and thought the requirement that | live alone in the forest with little human contact wouldn't be bad. l can walk to Gully to buy groceries and warmer clothes, borrow library books and make deliveries. They told me to stay out of restaurants, churches, meetings and the like. I didn't expect to be talking to anyone out here."

Ty suddenly remembered the scrap of matchbook cover. "Are you Nirvana?"

"How did you know?" asked a startled Nirvana.

"Your name was on a paper we found."

"We have ridden horses here before without seeing you," Patti said.

"I've moved several times because nobody was supposed to see me and I'm not to make a trail."

"Did The Secret Organization hire you?" Ty asked.

Nirvana shuddered. "You know too much. How did you find out about The Secret Organization? They want to remain secret."

"I think it was The Secret Organization that kidnapped and threatened to kill me," Ty answered grimly.

"Threatened to kill you? Kidnapped you? That isn't the sort of people I work for."

"What kind of people do you work for?"

"People who pay me very well. People who every week bring a package to a certain hollow tree so l can carry it to a hiding place for another of their employees. I'd better shut up. I'm telling you too much."

"Would that hiding place be the Old Historic Church in Gully?"

"You scare me."

"Why?"

"I'm not doing anything illegal. Going to that building at night with a locked box, then a couple days later going back for the empty box seemed like any easy job. Why are you here?"

"We saw the glint of your mirror or maybe it was the crystal and wondered if the glint was from a poachers rifle here before hunting season began."

"Oh, that's not me!"

"So I see."

"I have a warm sleeping bag, a tent that I only occupy if it is raining, warm clothes, a backpack, a beautiful night sky, fall leaf colors, library books to read, and wildlife to see. Have you ever looked at the night sky without any light pollution? It's wonderful! I don't know details about The Secret Organization or what is contained in lock-box I carry in the backpack. Please don't tell anybody I'm living in the public forest. My employers don't want any person to person contact with me in Vaca County or that I have any contact with their other employees here. When did you say hunting season begins? Will this forest be a dangerous place then?"

"If people make sound shots or shoot without knowing the appearance of the game they are licensed to shoot, yes. Younger hunters are required to take a hunter safety course in order to get a license. Older hunters should already know how to hunt safely. Deer, elk, moose, bear and cougar are the game that will be hunted. My boss used to have a buckskin horse that was shot by someone who thought she was a game animal."

"I've seen deer and elk, but never the other big game. Mostly I see chipmunks, porcupines, badgers, birds, weasels, garter snakes, butterflies, dragonflies, mosquitoes and flies."

"What do you know about your employer?"

"That every week my pay is in cash held to the lock-box by a rubber-band. The way here from Maryland was by train. The ticket was mailed to me at my parent's home just before they were deported. I got the job by answering a newspaper ad and was hired over the phone. I've never seen my employer. A man talked to me and interviewed me over the phone. Jobs are scarce, so I felt fortunate."

"Did the ad say Secret Organization?"

"No. There wasn't any name in the ad. One envelope that had my pay in it had Secret Organization scribbled on the outside. Other than that I've never seen or heard that name."

"How will you pay social security and income taxes?"

"I hadn't thought about taxes."

"Naive."

"What does that mean? I was born in the United States, so I'm a citizen, but my parents aren't. They are Asians that were here illegally. They were deported. At the library I use Skype to talk with my parents in Thailand. My choices to make a living were limited. Forced prostitution was the only option for most twelve-year-olds. I avoided that by taking this job. I just turned thirteen."

Ty had seen that she was young, had the slant eyes of an oriental and a darker shade of skin than his or Patti's. He knew he was beginning to feel sorry for her, but knew it wasn't sympathy she needed. The words on the matchbook cover scrap haunted him. What should he do?

"Nirvana, what would you like us to do?" Patti asked.

"Please don't tell anyone I'm here."

"It will get cold this winter, "Patti said. "You can live in my apartment in Gully starting the day hunting season begins, if I get permission from my landlord. I not only won't tell The Secret Organization, but also wouldn't know how if I wanted to. Hunting season begins the first of next month."

"My boss sent us here to find out what he saw flash in the light. Do I tell him it was a mirror or a crystal? I'm not inclined to lie to that man. We saw the light flash too."

"Would he keep my secret?" "Who knows? I doubt it. The Gully police are the people he would tell first, I think."

"The police? Why them? Please don't tell your boss you saw me and talked with me."

"Did you go to school?" Patti asked to ease the tension.

"Yes, that's how I know English. Tell your boss you saw a mirror in the woods. You did."

"Okay," Ty answered.

"You probably wondered about my name Nirvana. It means enlightenment, a state of spiritual awakening or supreme bliss, and that isn't how I feel now."

"I'll just have to pay more rent for my apartment when you move in with me for the winter. I'll tell you how much your share will be when I find out."

"I will miss living in this forest."

"Just for hunting season and while it's below zero cold, then."

"I appreciate the offer and will take you up on it. My next move will be near the bee hives I saw below the rocky ledge above us."

"The forest fence is between the ledge and the hives."

"Yes, it is. You can find me there unless I'm at the store or library. I borrowed this Christian Bible from the library because I wanted to compare Christianity with Buddhist beliefs. Here it is in my backpack."

Nirvana got out the Old King James Bible she had checked out of the Gully Library. "I'm puzzled by the differences and similarities between Buddhism and what I read in the Bible. Buddha founded Buddhism and taught four noble truths. His name was Siddhartha Gautama and his religion was an offshoot of the Hindu religion. The four noble truths are first: Everything leads to suffering. I suppose that my being cold when I must make deliveries at night is part of my suffering. Second: Desire or greed causes suffering. I have desires, but I'm not greedy. Third: Eliminating desire and greed eliminates suffering. So get rid of your desires. 1 even read that the tenth commandment in Exodus 20 of the Bible is Thou shalt not covet. Fourth Buddha taught that the pathways of enlightenment are open to anyone who lives morally and meditates. Buddha decided what was moral and what wasn't. I don't know where he got that information. A difference I found was where Matthew 6:7 says, 'when ye pray, use not vain repetitions as the heathen do: for they think that they shall be heard for their much speaking.' Psalm 1:2 says, 'In His law doth he meditate day and night.' Buddhists meditate by repeatedly reciting a mantra. It makes more sense to me to think about what I read in the Bible than to repeat any mantra over and over. This job leaves a lot of time for reading, so I have read this whole Bible and started over again. I wrote down references to look at more and I've started from Genesis again. Something that puzzles me is that we know where Buddha's body is in his grave, but the Bible says Jesus came back to life, that He took up His life again after three days and three nights in the grave and was seen by as many as 500 people after His resurrection. Jesus claimed to be God. He must be God to rise from the dead."

"Why were you named Nirvana?"

"My Buddhist parents must have thought Nirvana was a good name for their baby girl. In the library I use Skype to communicate with them. They are grateful I wasn't forced into prostitution. In Thailand that would have happened."

"I am appalled. That must be why your parents came to the United States illegally when you were expected."

"Yes."

"We won't tell anyone you are here, right Patti?"

"I won't tell and I do expect you to live with me as soon as I get permission for two to live in my apartment. The landlord will be happy to grant permission, because that will mean higher rent for him."

"I like it here, but you are most gracious and I will take you up on the offer during cold months."

"Bye now. See you soon."

"Don't forget to tell nobody I'm here."

As Ty and Patti rode to ranch headquarters, Ty mulled over his report to Cal whom he knew wouldn't just accept that a mirror was what he saw flash.

Chapter 11

Cal and Ty drove to the auction yard in Ute Creek the next morning after Ty fed the calf milk replacer. They would be there when the cattle entered the sale ring. Kyle would feed the calf until they returned.

As they sat watching the auction, Ty overheard a man who was obviously a novice. He looked behind him and saw Skeet and Benton. Skeet was talking.

"I hired Sid to replace Sonny because he has lived in Vaca County all his life and worked with cattle and fences."

"When does he start?"

"Sid, Dieter and Rodney are supposed to start fixing Fenner Place fences today. Closing hasn't happened yet, but we were told we could go ahead with repairing the fence and corrals before snow flies and the ground is frozen. Sid told me snow will knock down some fence, but this fall they can repair the corrals and some fencing in the more sheltered parts of the ranch."

Is that where you will send the cattle we buy today?"

"No, they will go to Frank Courtler's meadow and eat the hay we bought there. Frank wants their manure on his meadow."

"How are we going to feed the hay?"

"What do you mean?"

"The snow will get deep. We will need either a team of horses and harness to pull a hay sled or a track tractor to pull the sled. Horses cost less and I know how to drive a team. Frank has a horse drawn hay sled we can rent."

"How many cows can we feed?"

The bull will need at least 30 pounds of hay daily. A bred cow will eat 20 to 30 pounds and a team of horses will need 60 pounds for both of them. A small bale like Frank sold you weighs 60 to 65 pounds. The amount of hay Frank's meadow produced will feed 35 pregnant cows, the bull and a team for five months."

"We will have to brand the cattle and horses. I see there are three brands to be auctioned today. Branding can be done here before we truck the livestock."

"The nicest brand for sale today is a two character open brand that comes with branding irons."

"What does open mean?"

"There is no closed place that causes skin to die if an opening isn't left in the branding iron. Of the other two brands for sale, one has a closed D, but the irons have a cut in the D so the skin won't die. The third brand doesn't have any irons."

"We will bid on the best brand and hope to have the highest bid."

"All the cows will sell before the brands do."

"The sale sheet lists bred cows with words like smooth mouth cow, heifer-mate, heiferette, broken mouth cow and a fill. What do those terms mean?"

64

"A smooth mouth has no teeth and a broken mouth doesn't have all of her teeth. In a complete dispersal auction we could buy younger cattle, but here the only young cattle will be heifers so small the owner didn't want them. We can get a calf or two out of the older cows. If we buy any young cows, we better buy a calf puller. Some older people were born with forceps pulling them out of their mothers. A calf puller is similar. C- Section is used now for humans that are too big for their mothers and sometimes a veterinarian must C-Section a cow. We don't want small cows that will need a C-Section."

"The first cattle are in the ring."

Several groups of cattle went into and out of the ring while Skeet and Benton remained quiet. After a while Benton bid on twenty cows that a preg check showed they should calve in May. Benton gave the highest bid and the corporation Skeet worked for became the owner of Cal Grayson's late Angus and Hereford cows. It happened so fast that Ty saw the confusion on Skeet's face after the cows left the ring.

"That's not all 35, so we will watch for others due to calve in May," Benton said.

Ty and Cal watched too.Some of Cal's small heifers would be sold today. After those came into the ring and went to their new owner, Ty and Cal left.

"More cattle will sell tomorrow, so I've reserved a motel room with two beds. Now we have time to look at some scenery. That okay with you?"

"Sure." Ty wondered that his boss asked him. Cal gave the orders and Ty wasn't about to deviate from those again. Even so, he enjoyed some beautiful fall colors, snowcapped mountains and unusual rock formations. One formation looked like the eye of a needle, only much larger.

"Twenty of your cows, the ones due in May, were bought by Skeet, the man who hit Sonny Calhoun in the jaw the night he died," Ty said.

"Wasn't Skeet one of the men who held you hostage?"

"I think he was there, but since I was blindfolded and didn't recognize his voice, that is only a guess. My guess is based on the fact a bull was in the same barn or whatever building we were in, and it might have been the Pinzgauer bull I saw in the Calhoun homestead barn. No proof, just speculation."

"Would you recognize any of the kidnappers if you heard their voice?"

"I think so."

"Do you suspect that was the bull stolen from Canada?"

"Yes, but just suspicion, not proof."

A restaurant served a meal Ty enjoyed and he slept well on a comfortable bed. It would be afternoon that slaughter cattle began to sell. Ty went with Cal to a store that sold bee-keeping supplies, then to lunch at the auction restaurant. They watched the culls sell, including the mother of Ty's fall calf who was there because she was thought to be open (not pregnant). Ty was in line with Cal, who waited to get this annual paycheck. It was relieving to finally be on the way home.

"I hope Kyle did a good job of feeding my calf." "You get to feed her tomorrow morning and for the next five or six months."

"Looking forward to doing that."

"Good. After you feed her and yourself, bring a lunch tomorrow. Wear the new bee suit I bought for you. We will take the honey supers and extract honey tomorrow after we prepare the hives for winter. There are bales of moldy hay to protect three sides of the hives. The south side will remain open. I have insulated boards to put under the top covers. It has a little vent to prevent moisture from killing bees inside the hives. If we get enough honey, I'll buy Internet labels that meet requirements to sell honey at farmers markets. Last time I inspected my hives, I saw a girl up by the outcropping of rocks. She was on the forest side of the fence, but it still seemed strange. I never did ask you about the shiny object you and Patti went to find. Could it have been something she had?"

Chapter 12

At the bee hives Cal weighed each hive to ensure that each had at least 60 pounds of honey in the two deep supers for the bees to eat during the winter. He took honey only from honey supers at the top of the hives that had enough honey for the bees. Honey supers with the frames inside were quickly covered with wet towels to prevent honey robbers such as wasps from getting any honey. Later Ty loaded these into the pickup. Cal and Ty found a lot of honey supers full of capped honey. The solar electric fence around the apiary was intact that had kept bears away from the hives. Most of the hives were alive and healthy, but one had only a few dead bees in small back to back clusters on two frames and no dead bees elsewhere.

"The queen must have swarmed again. When she swarmed in the spring, I caught the swarm. This was a fall swarm, if that's what happened. There aren't any dead bees on the bottom board or ground. Maybe Colony Collapse Disorder, whatever that is, caused this loss. There is one more hive. Let's get it open. I saved it for last because that one has concerned me for some time. A lot of dead bees have been carried out of hive three for a couple of months now and there were lots of dead bees on the ground. Dead bee removal has stopped and I've seen no live bees at the entrance for a week."

Ty removed the rock holding down the cover so a gust of wind couldn't blow it off. Cal removed the honey super with full frames of wildflower honey. Then he used his frame lifter to take out a middle frame. One side of it was almost covered with dead bees. No movement was seen. Further examination revealed Cal had lost the entire colony, but no varroa mites were found either on bees or on the bottom board where there were many dead bees.

"I guess that if a 33% loss is normal, loss of two colonies is better than average," Cal said. The look on his face said he hadn't wanted to lose any. Cal placed Api Guard on top of the bottom super frames after removing honey supers. Thymol form those disks would kill any varroa mites without harming the bees. Ty began to put six moldy hay bales around each living colony Cal had treated, two high on three sides, leaving the south side and entrance open.

Cal installed entrance reducers and mouse guards on hives with living bees. He let the smoker that was used slightly to calm agitated bees that were defending their hives, sanitize his hive tool. When they had finished, Ty reconnected the electric fence. Cal put a stopper in the smoker to kill the fire that produced cool smoke. Equipment was loaded into the pickup. Ty and Cal removed their bee suits.

"Let's go up to the ridge and see if the girl is still there," Cal said.

Ty walked silently behind Cal. Soon they saw Nirvana was sitting on the ground beside her tent with binoculars trained on them.

"Did you watch us work the bees?" Cal asked.

Nirvana answered nervously. "Yes."

Ty wondered if she thought he told Cal about her. He knew he hadn't.

"Why are you staying in the forest?" Cal asked.

Nirvana looked directly at Ty. He shook his head from side to side as he looked at her.

"I will be staying in town come the first of the month. I like it out here because the stars at night are beautiful to see. This is public property, so it is legal for me to be here. Hunters and cold are the reasons for spending the winter in Gully."

"Have you seen any bear?" Cal asked.

"No."

"Good."

"I've seen meteorites. The fall yellow leaves among the evergreen trees and red leaves on some bushes are very pretty. The service berries (pronounced sarvis) are good eating."

"Right. My wife makes service berry jam, and she made gooseberry pie last July. After frost she will make chokecherry syrup."

Ty relaxed, as the conversation between Cal and Nirvana was peaceful.

"We have other work to do. Would you like to watch us extract honey and have some?"

"Is that what you will do now?"

"Yes."

"I'd like that." Nirvana rose to her feet and prepared to go with them. She sat in the middle between Cal and Ty in the pickup. Cal and Ty used an electric uncapping knife, then to get any wax remaining by the frame edges he used a tool that looked like a small paint roller to scratch off the remaining wax. He and Cal put the wax in a pan. Later that would be melted. Soon Nirvana was helping unload honey supers and put frames of uncapped honey in the extractor.

When the extractor was full, Cal turned on the electric motor.

Ty made sure honey was running into the five-gallon bucket under the opening at the bottom of the extractor. When the bucket was almost full, he closed the extractor opening and put a clean food-grade bucket under the opening. Then Ty opened the extractor. He poured the honey from the bucket using a gate valve at the bottom of the bucket to pour honey into a stainless steel tank with a closed opening at the bottom. This bucket when emptied he put aside, ready to fill with more honey later.

Call turned off the extractor motor, opened the lid and began turning frames around to extract honey from the other side. Nirvana and Ty helped.

"I will take the extractor to a car wash to clean it tomorrow. The frame holders will be cleaned in the dishwasher tonight. Ty, I'll want you to wash holding the pressure wand and I'll add more quarters to keep the water running at the car wash."

By the time the job was finished, the day was late. Nirvana was invited to eat supper with them, but declined, saying she must walk home now. She refused a ride home, laughing.

"I walk to Gully and back twice a week. It's a much shorter distance to my tent." Ty watched Nirvana leave. Instead of walking to her tent, she was walking the ten miles toward the town of Gully. He wondered if she would go to the Old Historic Church. Taking binoculars, he was just in time to see her remove something from the dead tree beside the road. Lightning had burned out its core and left an opening. Ty thought of the charred wood that might rub black off on her. It wasn't a place he'd ever touched. Does The Secret Organization put something inside the tree for her to courier to the church? Is she careful not to get any black charred wood anywhere on herself? Soon Nirvana was out of sight and Ty's brother came into the room.

It was the first time Ty saw Kyle since he'd gone to the auction, so he said, "Thank you for feeding my calf."

"You just divide the price of her first steer calf by the total number of days she must be fed milk replacer and pay me for those two days."

"That will be at least 2 and a half years or longer."

"I know. You actually don't owe me anything. I enjoyed feeding her. She was eager to drink from a bucket by sucking on two of my fingers like you told me. We didn't need the bottle and nipple we don't have."

"Works, doesn't it?"

"Sure does. I get the next orphan calf."

"If Cal has his way, there won't be a next time."

"That's okay too. Although ranch work is okay, what I'd really like to do is go to college and I think I can win scholarships and work my way through with a job near the college."

"I like ranching, being a cowboy, training horses, roping cattle and all that ranching entails, even bee-keeping and fence fixing."

"Do you mean at the bee hives Cal has? I stay away from those so I won't get stung."

We took the honey supers without being stung. Cal bought me a new bee suit when we went to the auction. We extracted the honey. Cal bought legal honey labels so he can sell the honey at farmers markets."

"What will the bees eat this winter if you took the honey they worked so hard to get?"

Cal weighed each hive and left over 60 pounds of honey for the bees to eat this winter. We didn't take any honey from the hives that were boxes of bees installed in hives last spring."

Dedra came into the room. She said, "Supper's ready."

Ty ate eagerly. He was hungry, but even more than food he wanted to spend the evening with Patti. Would she have learned more from Marci? Would Don and Melanie Marshall recover? He drove to Patti's apartment in Gully.

"Kraken de News gave Sonny Calhoun's autopsy findings," Patti said.

"What did they write?"

"The autopsy found that Sonny was murdered, but not by Skeet's blow to his jaw. That just knocked him to the floor. It was poison in a cigarette that killed him."

"Cigarettes poison smokers over the long haul. It would be years before his lungs were black and cancer tumors caused his years of sickness, then death."

"Here is what the article in the newspaper said: 'It wasn't tar and nicotine that killed Sonny Calhoun. That would take years off his length of life and cause a miserable painful death. A mixture of TCE (trichloroethanol) and cyanide so soon after he smoked a cigarette outside the Saddle Sore before coming inside caused a quick death. That poison was injected though the unopened pack and into a cigarette with a hypodermic needle. Forensic discoveries didn't tell who did the injecting or when. Cyanide would cause death quickly if ingested and almost as fast if smoked."

"Where could that cigarette pack have been before Sonny put it in his pocket?"

"The police have undoubtedly wondered about that."

"Could it have been in a carton in the store?"

"Needle holes were in the pack. Nothing in this newspaper article indicates that a carton of cigarette packs was involved or that a random target was in some twisted mind."

"Does it say there was more than one needle hole in the pack."

"Yes, so there must have been more than one poisoned cigarette."

"I suppose the rest of the pack was still in Sonny's shirt pocket."

"Likely."

"Sonny smoked outside the restaurant, then had time to enter and sit with Skeet and Benton in a booth.

Do you remember how long after that he fell to the floor?"

"Not long. We aren't the detectives working on this murder," Ty said.

"The police questioned us because we were eyewitnesses. They always want any tip that is important in a homicide investigation."

"We told them what we saw."

"The connection between Skeet and Sonny, Skeet and the kidnapping, Skeet buying the Fenner Place, Skeet and the Frank Courtler Ranch connection with Melanie Marshall being Frank's daughter, all have a common thread: Skeet."

"Don't forget Skeet and buying Cal's late to calve cows, or Nirvana taking something to place under the stairs at Old Historic Church."

"Nirvana is the girl we saw in the forest." Patti said.

"Yes, and she doesn't want us to mention her to anyone, but you were with me when we found her. Cal saw her himself, so l didn't have to decide how to tell him about her mirror."

"Rodney picked up the package from Old Historic Church when we were there with George."

"He did and I'm pretty sure he was one of the kidnappers. It must have been Skeet who gave Rodney's sandwich to me, saying Rodney was too fat."

"Rodney is too fat."

"We owe our lives to whoever didn't close that stock trailer door properly. That could have been Rodney."

"There were four men on the airplane. Sonny wasn't with them then."

"Maybe he was already in Gully with his parents."

"Probably. Not to change the subject, but Don and Melanie Marshall are out of the hospital. Marci told me.

Don has a cast on his arm and is doing as well as a one armed man can. Melanie was warmed slowly and recovered from her hypothermia. Duane is back to work bringing beetle kill pine logs out of the forest, down the river and to the lumber mill Don works for."

"I definitely did want to know they were okay."

"Could the kidnappers have wanted a ransom from the lumber and firewood industry?"

"Your guess is as good as mine, but I got the impression The Secret Organization gave Skeet and his employees all the money needed for renting a plane and helicopter, buying the Fenner Place and cattle. Who is The Secret Organization anyway and where do they get the money?"

"All I know about The Secret Organization is what I heard on the train. It is an organization that wants to end cattle ranching and all human use of animals."

"But Skeet bought cattle."

"That is a Cover-up."

Chapter 13

"Where have you been?" George asked when Ty answered the phone.

"The last place was feeding my calf."

"Your calf?"

"A lot has happened since the last time we talked. Cal gave me an orphaned calf. Twice a day I feed her milk replacer. She drinks it eagerly out of a bucket and wags her tail as she does."

"Have you named her?"

"Her ear tag number is 13359. That's her name. She was born last to Cal's number 359 mother cow in 2013, so at a glance we know how old she is."

"What color is she?"

"Black and white. The white is on her tail-head because her sire was Pinzgauer, mostly black with a white tail-head. Her mother a black Angus cow."

"Why was she an orphan?"

"Her mother was a cull cow and sold at auction because she was open, or at least we thought so. The calf was born in September. Cows Cal keeps in his herd have calves in April. He sold those due in May. He didn't know any would be born later unless there was a surprise late in June."

"What are you doing tomorrow?"

"We are going to split beetle kill logs for firewood. The dead trees were cut down and covered with plastic to kill pine beetles. The logs that were too small to make furniture are split and what isn't used as firewood to heat ranch buildings, Cal sells. There are a lot of beetle kill lodge pole pines on this ranch including the forestland Cal leases for pasture. We are working in the forest first because work there must end when hunting season begins. There's many more in other forestland and on other ranches. I hope that when Patti sold the Fenner Place to Skeet, she told him that the first thing they need to do is cut down beetle kill trees and put plastic over the logs before the snow falls."

"I saw Skeet and his cronies in Mike's Bar."

"That figures. You ought to be spiting logs for firewood. It's work I like."

"More than riding horses?"

"Now, don't go overboard."

"I thought you'd like to hear what Skeet said to Benton."

"Why would I want that gossip?"

"Because there was talk about four stolen horses. You told me Cal's old mare Dolly was stolen."

"Now you're talking. Did they say where she is?"

"Skeet and Benton left to see if four stolen horses are on the Frank Courtler meadow with the cattle he bought at an auction."

PART II

Chapter 14

"We only bought 27 cows at the auction. The Fenner Place should run 150 after all the fences and corrals and waterholes are repaired. Where do we get more, Benton?" Skeet asked.

"There might be a dispersal sale. I'll watch for ads. We will need to have a bull for each twenty to 25 cows. The one we have should be fine for 27 in the meadow. For this winter, the sale next Wednesday will have some Churro sheep. The Navajo people used them for both milk and meat. Now they need more herds and could buy from us if we are successful when we bid on them. There aren't too many for us to feed this winter. The main problem with sheep is that there are plenty of coyotes that like to eat lamb and mutton. We will need a sheepherder if we get sheep."

"Can you be a sheepherder?"

"Yes, I could watch the sheep and Sid take care of the cattle."

"We didn't get a brand at the auction. That's just as well. I got a message from The Secret Organization that they want one with two S's in the brand."

"We need to keep the paperwork that shows ownership of those 27 cows in a safe place. I looked in the brand book at the library for brands with an S because your first name begins with S. A lot of brands contain S. One is SSSS.

Another has three S's backwards. If we don't buy a brand that is for sale, we can make up one that isn't used. It will have to be a three-character brand because all of the one and two character brands are taken. SSS or having an S facing backwards might be accepted. If we use only S, only one branding iron will be needed to make the brand. Of-course we would want more than one S so a brand would always be hot or cold enough to use. If we get all black or red cattle, freeze branding will work because the hair turns white. Nitrogen is used the make the iron cold. A smaller brand is used on horses and freeze branding is best for them. White and yellow hair has to have a hot brand so it can be seen."

"I hear horses will sell Wednesday too," Skeet said.

"That is a sale mostly for horses that have a bad problem. We don't want most horses that sell at that auction. There is a draft horse auction that we should attend next Saturday. Good ready to use teams will be there," Benton said.

"What about riding horses?"

"Those can wait until next spring. Any riding we need to do this winter can be done bareback on the draft horses."

"What about the four horses Rodney and Dieter stole? You refused to ride yours."

"Rodney and Dieter were wrong to steal. The horse handed to me was lame. That is painful enough without my weight causing him more pain. The horse Dieter got on was blind. A blind horse can become balky and refuse to move when you need movement quickly. The one you rode was old and thin and could only move slowly. The other horse had bad conformation and you saw that Roman nosed swaybacked horse buck Rodney off. Those horses should be returned to their owners pronto."

"They are at Frank Courtler's ranch."

"And I wasn't happy to see them. Let me pick good horses. It takes as much feed for a worthless horse as for a useful horse. Only kill buyers and possibly some children would want those four."

Rodney and Dieter came into Mike's Bar as Skeet and Benton talked. Skeet frowned at Rodney.

"Rodney, come over to our table. You and Dieter must return those stolen horses to their owners today."

"Why?"

80

"Your job isn't to question my orders. No drinking. Just get the horses into the trailer and take them home. Dieter, you help Rodney."

Dieter frowned.

"I suppose you thought I couldn't ride the horse that bucked with me. I will try again with a saddle. I couldn't stay on bareback is all," Rodney said.

"You are not to ever get on that stolen horse again," Skeet said.

"Let's go," Dieter said. "All four horses are what he said, stolen, so it isn't just about bucking."

"I am unhappy with Rodney anyway," Skeet said. The sheriff knew where he hid the stolen Jeep. He thought the Calhoun homestead was a very remote place where it would stay hidden in the trees. Fortunately, the owner got it back without a wreck ruining the vehicle. To look legit, none of us must steal."

"I never was sure about the bull from Canada. You did pay for him, didn't you?" Benton asked.

"Don't ask questions, Benton. You have a job because you know livestock. Sid knows livestock too, and he is a lot younger."

"As you say, boss."

"The police or sheriff are going to question me because Rodney hid the Jeep in the wrong place. I don't need that to happen, but it will and I'm not in a good mood."

Benton said no more. He ate the delicious steak Mike's wife had cooked expertly. Skeet didn't eat much, but guzzled his second beer. When it was gone, Skeet said, "Let's go. I want to see if those four horses are gone."

Arriving at the Courtler barn, they were in for an unwanted surprise. The stolen horses were nowhere to be seen, but sheriff deputies arrested both of them as horse-thieves.

"I didn't steal any horses or anything else," Benton protested.

"I didn't either," Skeet lied.

81

"You are both coming down to headquarters," the deputy said as he guided them into a squad car. The men were taken to separate interrogation rooms.

"Skeet, tell me why there were four stolen horses on the meadow you rented."

"I don't know."

"Are you telling me you haven't been there?"

"No. I'm telling you I didn't steal those horses."

"But you admit the horses were there." Skeet hesitated.

"Don't get smart with me. Answer my questions."

"I saw the horses and even rode one before I knew they were stolen. I told the thieves to take them home to their owners," Skeet said.

"Who were the thieves you told to take the horses home?"

"I told Rodney to put those horses in the stock trailer and return them to the pastures where he stole them."

"Rodney. What is his last name?"

"Simms."

"What makes you think Rodney Simms stole the horses?"

"He is a thief."

"How do you know?"

"He knew where to take those horses. I came to Frank Courtler's ranch to see if he did like I told him to."

"Don't you know where they came from?"

"No."

"The brand inspector took the horses to the sale barn at the fairgrounds and Rodney Simms to jail. Dieter Penzwich was taken to jail too and there was an outstanding warrant for his arrest. If the horses are branded, the owners of the brands will be contacted."

"I don't think all of them were branded. What happens then?"

"Brands are a return address for livestock. Estray laws say the brand inspector has authority to move unbranded livestock found outside limits of its usual range or pasture to move such animal to a safe and practical place within the immediate vicinity to be held during the legal advertising period. My job isn't to explain the law to you. I have you here for questioning. There are other questions I have for you. Why did you hit Sonny Calhoun the night he sat in a booth with you at the Saddle Sore Inn?"

"I didn't kill Sonny! I needed Sonny. He was a good employee. I'm not a murderer, but if I was, Sonny would not be the victim."

"Let me repeat my question. Why did you hit Sonny?"

"We had a disagreement. I needed to show who was in authority."

"And you do that with your fist?"

"I wish it had been done some other way. I'm sorry I slugged him."

"What would be a better way to show authority to an employee?"

"Talk calmly and definitely, leaving no room for discussion."

"What did you disagree about?"

"Sonny said not to buy the Fenner Place because it was the worst ranch in Vaca County. I'd read the prospects that Gully Real Estate put on the Internet. It said the ranch was priced as a fix up and when the work was done the ranch could run 150 mother cows. I wanted Sonny to help with the work."

"So you didn't want Sonny to question your decisions."

"That's right."

"Who was the older man with you?"

"Benton. You brought him in here with me."

"Is Benton your employee?"

"Yes. He has expertise with livestock."

"Did Benton help you steal the Pinzgauer bull that was in the barn on the Frank Courtler Ranch?"

"No! That bull wasn't stolen."

"Do you have the sale papers? His brand belongs to a ranch in Canada that raises purebred bulls and reported a prize bull stolen from a big livestock show."

"Not with me."

"Where are they?"

"I lost them."

"Why is there a bulletin to watch for a prize bull of his coloring and size stolen from a show?"

"I wouldn't know."

"The brand inspector took custody of that bull. You must produce the sale paper to get him back." Skeet was silent.

"There is something else. What do you know about a white 4wd Jeep Wrangler?"

"Am I supposed to know something? I came here by airplane, not in a Jeep."

"Rodney Simms was seen driving the white Jeep on an old wagon trail. You do know Rodney Simms. He is one of your employees, isn't he? Didn't you tell him to drive that Jeep?"

Without giving an answer, Skeet looked down at his shoes and wondered what else the Sheriff deputy knew. He'd expected to be questioned about the Jeep because it too was stolen and Rodney hadn't hidden it so it would never be found.

"Hit a nerve, did I. Your silence is answer enough. You are being held for assault, and theft."

"The deputy left the room with the door locked. The Secret Organization will bail me out, Skeet thought. At least I wasn't charged with kidnapping. The door opened and two deputies walked in. "There is another charge. Kidnapping. Book him into the jail."

Chapter 15

Skeet called Dieter and asked him to get a message to The Secret Organization that he needed a lawyer and to be bailed out of jail. That was his one phone call, then he waited and waited. Several days later an attorney came to his jail cell.

"Before I make bail, you need to tell me what this is about."

"It wasn't my idea to do anything I'm charged with. I didn't murder Sonny Calhoun. I didn't kidnap anyone. I didn't steal horses."

"Or a valuable bull? Or a Jeep? You would deny all of the charges, of-course. What I need is information from which to make a defense."

"Bail me out before we talk."

"Bail is set very high. I'm surprised you can be bailed out."

"How high?"

"Three million."

"Whew! I didn't..."

"Never mind. Who is in charge while you are here?"

"I guess Dieter is, but he isn't, well he isn't completely honest and maybe he is still in jail."

"And you are completely honest?"

"I told my men there was to be no more stealing after I found out about the horses."

"What about the kidnapping charge?"

"Rodney got that going. It wasn't my idea."

"So you aren't in control of your employees. We expected you to be in charge."

"I am in charge when with the men."

"And when you aren't with them, you still are expected to be in charge, the boss."

"Are you going to post bail?"

"That hasn't been decided. Who else is there? Someone who is more trustworthy than either Dieter or Rodney needs to fill in. Don't you have a new employee, Sid? What about him?"

"As far as I know, Sid is honest, trustworthy and knowledgeable."

"Do you think he could control the men?"

"He is younger than Dieter, in fact the same age as Rodney. He can build fence and handle livestock, but I don't know if he can handle men, especially since he is the newest employee."

"Doesn't sound like anyone could be boss, but Benton is old enough and has been with you longer."

"Benton knows livestock. I'm not so sure he knows men."

"My time is up. See you next time I'm allowed to visit. I will be in contact with all of your men and decide who is in charge, maybe me."

A week later Skeet was bailed out of jail and released at midnight, very thankful to be out of that rough environment. He must appear in court, but the arraignment was a ways off. Skeet walked to his hotel room and went to sleep. A knock on his door woke him the next morning. After breakfast at the Red Fox, he went with The Secret Organization attorney who had bailed him out of jail, to the Frank Courtler Ranch. Only Benton and Sid were there, but they were busy as Benton drove a team of horses pulling a hay sled loaded with hay and Sid pitched off bales after he cut off the twine holding the hay together. Twenty-seven Angus and Hereford cows gathered around the hay Sid pitched onto clean snow and ate eagerly. Skeet and the attorney watched this scene, enjoying the serene setting, life as it should be Skeet thought. No more crime for me. I like the good life instead of the criminal I've been.

The attorney startled Skeet out of his thoughts. "Arraignment has been scheduled for two weeks from today. I must return to Maryland, but will be back to go to court with you. You are in charge as boss of Benton and Sid. I fired Dieter and Rodney. Rodney wouldn't obey orders and although Dieter worked hard when the Fenner Place fence was being repaired, he was worthless here now that snow has fallen above 8000 feet. Dieter can be rehired to work at the Fenner Place if he wants the job next spring. Benton and Sid do the job very well. You will mostly be tending to the water tank, filling it, making sure the tank heater is keeping ice off the water and getting food for the three of you. The truck and trailer are legal, fortunately, so only the white Jeep, red car, and bull Rodney stole are gone along with those two men. The Secret Organization doesn't condone any more illegal activity here. Do not leave Vaca County for any reason. The truck will carry the three of you when you pick up packages from The Secret Organization or get food. You should also be repairing the house at the Fenner Place this winter so all of you can live there instead of at a hotel. There are no other reasons to be away from this ranch before I return. Understand? The attorney got into his rented car and drove away.

Skeet wondered just who put those packages under the stairs at Old Historic Church. The courier is from The Secret Organization, but I have no idea who he is.

Skeet watched him go, then watched Benton and Sid finish feeding the cattle. He helped them take the harness off the horses and hang it in the barn. Sid put the team in barn stalls to eat their hay from the manger. "The horses would drive the cows away from their hay. When both horses and cows have finished eating, I will turn the horses out with the cows. Benton sure bought a nice Clydesdale team and good cows," Sid said. "It's nice you are back, Skeet, although we were doing fine. It's especially great to not have Rodney dreaming up mischief or wanting to spend time in the bar drinking. I miss Dieter, though."

"I will be arraigned in court in two weeks. Then I will still be out on bail. There is to be no more illegal activity, so I'm glad Rodney is gone. I will miss Dieter too. Maybe he will come back in the spring."

"It is time for dinner. Benton and I have been eating at the Red Fox. Let's go there now."

"The Red Fox serves much better food than the jail."

"Hello Skeet," Benton said as he walked toward the men. "The two of us will be sharing one hotel room. The attorney stopped renting the room you shared with Rodney."

"Fine with me," said Skeet. "Have you picked up any packages at Old Historic?"

"No, the attorney was the only one who went there. On nights there should be a drop, you do want one of us to bring it to the hotel, I suppose. The only thing we expect is something telling us when his plane lands in two weeks. He left enough money for us to pay the hotel bill and eat for two weeks."

PART III

Chapter 16

Ty continued to cut down beetle kill pines, put big logs in a pile for furniture makers, cover those with plastic to kill beetles and cut then chop smaller logs into firewood, then cover those with plastic. Evenings when Patti didn't have real estate to show, the pair rode horses together, Ty on Cowgirl and Patti on Cowman.

"Nirvana is an interesting roommate. She doesn't talk about her job at all and avoids all other residents in the apartment building. Twice a week she goes out for a walk during the day then at night goes out again. She's gone about the same amount of time every trip. She likes to talk about the differences between Buddhism and what she has read in the Bible. She has read much more of the Bible than I ever have."

"I haven't read any of the Bible. I suppose I should."

"Marci told me the experience Duane had before you joined the hostages in the Courtler barn."

"What did she say?"

"Duane and Marci had taken their two children to the babysitter, then waited together for a carpool ride to Don and Melanie's house in Shale for a potluck get acquainted dinner. A red car arrived and Duane got in. The car sped away while Marci was still locking the house. She was frantic. The car didn't return for her, so she called Marshall's and couldn't get an answer. She called the church and got a recording. She called the Pastor and got another recording. She tried Marshall's again. The phone rang four times, then went dead. The thought that crossed her mind was, is Duane dead too? Next she called her mother. Marci uses a lot of Bible verses in her conversation. That's what got me to reading God's word with Marci when we are on break. Evidently her mother does too. Her mother told her to remember Philippians 4:6 "Be anxious for nothing but in everything by prayer with thanksgiving let your requests be made known to God." Then her mother said, "Let's pray right now over the phone." They did. Marci thanked her mother and hung up. She was calmer and dialed the Telephone Company to report Marshall's dead phone. A recording told her the business hours. She said she was thankful God didn't have office hours. Using her smart phone again, she called the police. She was told they couldn't do anything unless they were sure a crime had been committed. After 24 hours she could file a missing person's report."

"Did she do that?"

"Yes, but before 24 hours went by and before she got the children from the babysitter, she took her son's softball bat with her in their car to Marshall's house."

Ty and Patti let their horses gallop on the flat. When the ranch road resumed winding uphill they slowed their mounts to a walk and continued talking.

"What did she find at Marshall's house?' Ty asked.

"Most of the people invited to the dinner were there milling about. Don and Melanie Marshall weren't there and neither was her husband. There was a dead dog in the back yard with lots of fresh red blood and a bloody kitchen knife. There was a smart phone in the garage and another in the kitchen and the wires to their landline had been cut. The police were there."

A beautiful orange sunset graced the western sky, so Ty said, "It's time to turn back so we'll get to headquarters before dark."

Patti continued, "Marci asked the police about her husband. They added his name to their notes. That was all she learned before going to the babysitter's house for her children."

"Whoever kidnapped the Marshall's also killed their dog. The people I overheard on The Secret Organization train threatened to kill me. It could be that they killed Sonny Calhoun, but why was Sonny killed and why was there a kidnapping?"

"It seems more and more likely that Skeet, Benton, Dieter and Rodney are Secret Organization employees and we know Nirvana is a Secret Organization employee."

"I wonder if having Nirvana live in your apartment this winter puts you in danger."

"I doubt it."

"I hope not."

"Tomorrow Cal said we would empty metal water tanks and turn them over so freezing won't burst them this winter."

"What will the cattle and horses drink? Rivers freeze over."

"We moved the cattle onto the meadows that have heated concrete water tanks. I check those daily."

"Well, we better turn our horses loose and head for bed. Hunters will be here tomorrow."

Chapter 17

Ty sat down with his cat on his lap to look at the newspaper before going to bed. ASCS offered an emergency livestock feed program controlled by the Federal Government and financed by taxpayers. USDA had released county price support rates for these years' crops. The Forest Service had issued burdensome conditions, terms and fees for renewal of special use permits for reservoirs, canals and ditches whose end use is water for agricultural irrigation. Special use permits could be converted to permanent easements for irrigation and stock watering. Permanent easements would be terminated if the water were used for anything else. Upon issuance of the easement, right of way grants would be relinquished.

Ty knew Colorado is a state where the doctrine of prior appropriation governs allocation of water. Cal would assert his vested right of way grants for his ditches carrying water from forestland to deeded land. Some of Cal's time must be spent in activity Ty knew Cal considered unproductive bureaucratic red tape.

The paper had a front-page picture in color of a large bull elk. The hunters who would be in place at sunrise in the morning on Cal Grayson's ranch had arrived, parking their campers and horse trailers in the headquarters yard.

Their hunting horses were in Cal's corrals and barn. All had gone to bed early. Most would turn in the heads of elk they killed to the Division of Wildlife for testing to be sure the meat was safe to eat. The paper gave the address and directions to the place. Brains of some elk were infected with a disease similar to bovine spongiform encephalopathy (mad cow disease). So far neither spooky disease causing holes in brains had been found on Cal's ranch. Cal asked every hunter on his ranch to pay the Division of Wildlife to test any elk they killed. Those who wanted taxidermy would have to find out if they could get the trophy heads back that tested negative. Hunters were warned to look for deer ticks infected with Lyme disease. Not all ticks would carry this disease, but those who did must be removed quickly without burning the tick. Ticks would bite in dark areas where people often didn't look.

Ty thought of the wood ticks that could bite people who walked by sagebrush, mostly in June. Those ticks could carry Rocky Mountain Spotted tick fever. Ty read on although he was becoming sleepy. Elk and deer hunting brought over $40 million dollars to the Division of Wildlife the previous year. It was estimated that out of state hunters brought $600 million to Colorado's economy. Over 235,000 elk hunters killed at least 45,000 elk each year. Most of those killed would be bull elk. Few cow elk licenses were issued. There were only two ranches in Vaca County where no hunters were given permission to hunt. Gully Real Estate Company wanted prospective buyers to see live elk. The moose, deer, cougar and bear harvest was given less coverage. Ty turned the page, and found an article about his kidnapping. There was nothing Ty didn't already know. Ty also found the paper's update about the Sonny Calhoun murder. It said Skeet Grinwold was not a suspect. He put down the paper and looked out at the full hunter's moon as he headed towards bed.

The next morning was chilly. Ty put the orange hunting vest over his coat so it could be seen as he worked with water tanks. As Cal and Ty emptied water from the metal tanks and overturned them, leaving large rocks under the edges to keep them off the ground, they could hear several rifle shots.

"More No Trespassing signs are needed on our borders.

The hunters who paid me to hunt here don't want competition from unauthorized hunters," Cal said.

"Somebody already got an elk," Ty said.

Below they could see a horse carrying a halved gutted elk while led by the hunter.

"I can't tell from here which hunter filled a license already, but I'm not surprised that a license was filled on the morning of the first day. Elk become wary quickly and licenses will be harder to fill."

"The bolt closing the bottom of this tank is too tight for the wrench alone. Do you have any penetrating oil?"

"It's in the pickup, behind the driver's seat."

Ty went after the can. After using it he was able to get the bolt loose, letting water pour out. The day finished with three more tanks to empty the next day.

The next morning, Cowgirl wasn't sure those signs belonged on her back, so Ty took extra time getting her used to them. The signs were wired to fences, and then water tank work resumed. Ty had time to check the wellbeing of the cattle that afternoon. Ending the day without being so tired; he showered, put on clean dress clothes and drove to Gully.

Ty and Patti went to the evening church service at Gully Community Church for the first time. To their surprise, Skeet and Benton were also there. The uncomfortable feeling of being where he'd never been before left Ty after the service began.

"Take a hymn book from under the seat in front of you, then stand while we sing hymn 458."

Ty and Patti shared a hymnbook, but didn't do much singing. The song was unfamiliar. After the hymn as they sat, Ty heard Benton whisper to Skeet, "Why church?"

"We must look respectable," Skeet answered.

Ty took Patti home right after the service and went to bed soon after getting home. Ranch work would continue early in the morning. It seemed like work that must be done in the fall never ended.

He enjoyed the ride on Cowgirl that he took almost every day so she would be a well-trained horse by spring. When Cal examined the beehives and gave the bees more sugar syrup, Ty went with Cal, so they could be together on the next job, repairing a broken water line to a heated stock tank.

The next day Ty and Cal found a heifer with foot rot as they rode through the herd.

"It's time for Cowgirl to get some team-roping experience," Cal said. "I'll rope her head and then you rope her heels. You stay on your horse and teach her to keep the rope tight. I will get off while my horse keeps the head rope tightly and doctor her."

Cal used his bailing gun to shove sulfa pills down the heifer's throat, cleaned out her sorr hoof and put disluted iodine on it, then remounted his horse.

"Ask Cowgirl to go forward so the rope is loosened and falls from her heels at the same time as you remove my rope from her neck."

This wasn't easy, but Ty was very experienced at team roping from Cowman, so Cowgirl, who already knew ropes were okay and the heifer were the only new factors. It all happened as planned.

The heifer limped away as fast as she could with her sore front foot.

A week later when Ty and Patti were riding, they found a young cow that needed to be doctored for lump jaw. "This time it's your turn Cowgirl," Ty said to his horse. "Patti, do you want to rope the head or the heels?"

"Head," answered Patti and she did just that, catching the two-year-old heifer by the neck.

Ty roped both hind heels. The cow caught between the two tight ropes could only bawl. Ty jumped down, ordered Cowgirl to keep the rope tight and hoped she would. He was somewhat amazed when she backed to keep the rope tight instead of walking toward him as he went to the cow's head with a sharp knife and a razor. Quickly he shaved off hair on the lump. Then he slit the lump open, letting the pus drain out. Ty wiped the knife blade with some grass and put the sharp hunting knife back in the sheath carried on his belt.

"Patti, I'll take your rope off the cow's head when you ride forward as I lead Cowgirl forward so the cow can step out of my rope." Coordination was perfect and the angry cow moved quickly away from them, pus dripping from the wound.

"She will drain out and be like new."

"Right."

"I'll clean the knife better with soap and water, then rubbing alcohol when I get home."

"I suppose you'll clean the inside of the sheath with rubbing alcohol on a rag."

"I'd better." Ty smiled at Patti. She was the perfect girlfriend. It was time to take her home.

The next day Ty worked steadily, whistling as he welded in the shop with his dad.

"The rough ground wears out machinery in a hurry," his dad remarked.

"It's still good for another haying season and will be ready when we need it mid-July," Ty said.

"You are seeing a lot of Patti."

"I love her," Ty said.

"Your calf is growing like a weed."

"She eats eagerly, drinking milk the new milk cow gives."

"Did you try having her drink from the cow instead of from a bucket?"

"Yes, the cow didn't want a calf that wasn't hers, and we didn't have a hide to tie around the calf."

"Of-course not. The milk cow calf is still very much alive and fed like your calf. The milk from the dairy cow is better for the calf, I think, and plenty is left for the table."

"Buying a milk cow and milking her twice a day was my idea," Ty said. That Brown Swiss cow was tested for Tuberculosis so the milk would be safe.

"Still think buying a milk cow was a good idea?"

"Yes, even though I have more work to do and we have fresh milk for our cereal. Mother was used to pasteurized milk, so she's been heating it to 160 degrees and cooling it before we use the milk."

Chapter 18

Ty looked into the courtroom where he saw Skeet was dressed in a new black western suit fastened green cowboy shirt and pointed black cowboy boots for his trial. He sat quietly at the defendant's table beside his Secret Organization attorney who also wore a western suit. A pleasant innocent look covered Skeet's face as he waited for proceedings to begin.

Ty had been summoned as a prosecution witness. This meant he must milk his cow and feed his calf very early before driving to the courthouse in Shale. Court would let out in time for him to drive home and milk his cow and feed his calf just before dark. He sat outside in the hall with the other witnesses waiting for the call for him to enter the courtroom. He must not hear other witnesses testify.

Patti had to work, so she wasn't there. Neither were Kyle or Dedra, who had to attend school. His parents weren't there because they had to work. Ty

101

was instructed not to converse with Don and Melanie Marshall or Duane Dunbar, because they were also witnesses for the prosecution, as were the medical team who had cared for Don and Melanie. Sheriff deputies in the hall also stayed silent. Frank Courtler sat in the only high back chair, dozing.

Ty wasn't called to testify the first day of the kidnapping trial nor the second. He sat in the hall thinking about the work he would rather be doing. On the third day Ty was called to the stand. He was sworn in with his right hand held up and noticed the Holy Bible wasn't used. Questioning by the prosecution was easy, but when the defense questioned him, he felt attacked and shredded.

When the kidnapping phase of the trials Skeet was charged with was over, the prosecution gave their summation. Then The Secret Organization attorney gave a summation that tore down Ty's testimony again.

"Tyler Grenshaw shouldn't have even been with the people who were hostages in this kidnapping. He was an un-ticketed stowaway on an excursion train he never should have boarded. Harold Grinwold, also called Skeet, wasn't on that train, so he definitely didn't grab Tyler and kidnap him. Tyler didn't see Harold Grinwold at any time while he was a hostage who was where he never should have been, nosing into business that wasn't his. Tyler couldn't identify Harold Grinwold by sight, smell, touch, hearing or taste. He never should have been on that train. How about Don and Melanie Marshall and their new friend Duane Dunbar? Harold Grinwold didn't kidnap them either! He wasn't there when the Marshall's were kidnapped from the Marshall's home in Shale or Duane Dunbar from his home. He only learned about the kidnapping later. The four hostages were taken to the Frank Courtler barn that Harold Grinwold had rented for his livestock. He shouldn't ever have been implicated in a crime he didn't commit. He wondered why anyone was kidnapped and ordered the hostages removed from the Frank Courtler Ranch. The wrong man was charged with this crime."

The Secret Organization attorney sat down and the jury was sent to deliberate. Harold "Skeet" Grinwold was acquitted.

Chapter 19

"Did the jury decide that Skeet kidnapped you?" Cal asked Ty when he came to work the next morning.

"No, and he wasn't on the train where l was taken, so the jury was right about me."

"Today I want you to ride Cowgirl first. She hasn't been ridden for several days."

Ty was delighted. He knew ditch repair must be done, but having a reliable horse was important too. He caught and saddled the 15:1 hand tall mare, thinking she is just the right size for a ranch horse, likes roping, is cowy in that she keeps calves ahead of her so they don't go back to the place they last saw their mother's. She pay's attention and does as she is asked. She is fairly easy to catch too. She understood use of his weight, legs, reins and voice and wanted to please Ty. Ty sat on her with his weight in the stirrups instead of like a bag of salt. She liked that, but must learn to carry bags of salt to salt troughs. After a nice ride, Ty put a bag of salt on her saddle and tied it there. Leading Cowgirl from Cowman, he watched the puzzled Cowgirl learn something new. If there were a game damage season, she would also be ready to carry any cow elk he was licensed to kill.

The morning ride went by quickly. As ditches were repaired, Cal said, "I want you to fix up the cabin by the creek and make it livable. Insulation for that cabin is inside. The wiring must be installed first. And the plumbing. When it was a homestead cabin in the 1800's, there was no electricity or indoor plumbing. I've needed a good hunting and fishing cabin for a long time, and never had time. Before it snows, put sealer on the outside after caulking between logs. I'll have to buy sealer and the plumbing and wire next time I'm in the town of Elk Creek.I have to go there next week."

That evening Ty went to Gully and walked Skooter with Patti.

"Who had access to cyanide and TCE, Sonny's cigarettes and a hypodermic needle to put poison in those cigarettes?" Patti wondered.

"Various sizes of hypodermic needles with syringe are easily available at the hardware store for use in livestock," Ty said. "Cyanide and TCE, I have no idea."

"Some people who had access to Sonny's cigarettes would want him alive. Who might have a motive for wanting him dead?"

"TCE is used to clean metal parts," Ty said.

"So a garage or lawnmower or a clock and watch repairman could get it. Is it used in the machine shop at the ranch?'

"Not that I know of."

"Hydrogen cyanide is very toxic, although that depends on the dose. Some other cyanides aren't toxic. Cyanide can be gas, liquid or solid. To be injected, it must have been liquid," Patti said.

"Where did you find out all this stuff?"

"Internet." "What use does cyanide have?"

"An internal combustion engine produces cyanide. It is found in cigarette smoke. It is used in a gas chamber, in war, for suicide, murder, fumigation and gold mining," Patti said.

"That's a lot of uses, some industrial. There is gold mining nearby."

"There are other uses such as lowering blood pressure fast and an illegal catch of fish near coral reefs."

"So the hospital probably has cyanide, but there definitely aren't any coral reefs in this landlocked state."

"I'm trying to think of people with a bad motive that have access to those poisons and Sonny's cigarettes and don't think of anyone," Patti said.

"You might as well let detectives sort that out."

"Yes, of-course, but I do read mystery novels, who-done-it types."

"Those are novels. This is real life and death."

"The date wasn't long, just a connection Ty wanted to make often. As he drove home to the ranch, Ty wondered that Nirvana hadn't left the apartment to walk with them and decided that since it was a date she wouldn't have been comfortable with them. Or maybe, he mused, she feared being seen with other people because of instructions by The Secret Organization. Did they know she wasn't staying in the forest where it was cold in the winter?

Chapter 20

As Patti and Ty went on an evening horseback ride together, she looked worried. "Ty, last night Nirvana said she was going to the forest to look at the night sky because it was so pretty and there are too many lights in Gully. She said she would be back to the apartment later, after her drop at Old Historic Church was made. She never came home last night at all. This morning I told the Gully police I wanted to tell them about a missing person, but was told that since there wasn't any evidence of a crime, I'd have to file my report after 24 hours had elapsed unless Nirvana was found sooner. I've been at work all day, then when l got home, there was no indication that she'd used her bed or eaten anything."

"Let's ride into the forest and look for her."

"At night hunting isn't allowed, but we want to be there before sundown. It's too dark."

We will be on the ranch until after we reach the apiary. There is a gate into the forest nearby. I need to make sure the solar electric fence around the beehives is still working. Bears haven't hibernated yet."

"Okay. What about the ranch hunters?"

"All of them have filled their licenses and are gone."

"Look. A bull elk with a big rack is standing on the meadow below us." Patti pointed.

"He came out into the open when he felt safe. That animal is a wise old trooper who has survived many hunting seasons. I've seen him before."

"You recognize an elk?"

"I counted his horn points. There is one more on the right side than on the left."

Fall leaves had mostly fallen from trees and only evergreens retained their leaves. Cattle still grazed on the meadow grass that had re-grown after it was mowed or grew on ditch banks that never were mowed. No snow had fallen at this elevation yet. Ty and Patti rode in silence at a walk for several miles, just enjoying the quiet and contemplating Nirvana's whereabouts.

"Do you think Nirvana stayed in the forest or got something from the hollow tree and went to drop it off under the Old Historic Church steps? Is this one of her two courier nights?"

"Well, yes, she did plan to pick up the empty lock box yesterday, leave it in the hollow tree and take the other lock box to the hiding place under the stairs. The forest isn't a lot further than the hollow tree and she goes out at night. I'm concerned that she never returned to the apartment. It is even colder in the wee hours of the morning than it was when she moved into the apartment. Maybe she went missing after the drop in Gully."

"If you don't see her before 24 hours is gone, go ahead and file the report that she is missing."

"Ty, there is something I wanted to tell both you and Nirvana. During break at work Marci led me to Christ."

"What do you mean?"

"She asked me if I'd ever received Jesus as my Savior. I was puzzled, so she asked me if I would go to heaven."

"I said I hoped so."

"She said we could know for sure if we would be in heaven, then she asked me, 'If you stood before God and He asked why He should let me into His heaven, what would you answer?' and I said, 'I think the good things I've done outweigh the bad things I did."

"I think you are good enough. Don't worry about that. It's enough to wonder where Nirvana is."

"Marci said we can't get to heaven by being good because God's holy standard is perfection and nobody's perfect. God found every person guilty, none righteous, no not one, is the way the Bible puts it. Then after finding us guilty, God sentenced us to death. Then God Himself came down to earth as a baby born to a virgin, experienced all the temptations humans face as the God/man, only Jesus the Christ was without sin and paid our way to heaven on the cross. She said that if I agreed with God that I had sinned, believed that Jesus the Christ died to pay the penalty for my sin, was buried and arose from the dead, then called on Jesus to save me, He would save me, something I couldn't do for myself."

"You sound like Pastor Malluchi."

"He has said the same thing, but it took Marci Dunbar to convince me. I asked Jesus to save me and He did. Ty, I want you to be saved too."

"I know I've sinned, believe Jesus can save and so if I ask him to save me, will He?"

"Yes.Romans 10:13 says, "For whosoever shall call on the name of the Lord shall be saved.""

"I've thought about that ever since Sonny Calhoun's funeral. Yes, I do believe. Jesus save me right now."

"Do you know Jesus saved you?"

Ty smiled. "Yes, I do."

"I see vultures circling overhead. Do you suppose some hunter wounded an animal and didn't find the carcass when he died?" "The vultures that were circling above something have flown down on the forest side of the fence. It's getting on towards dark. Let's look before it gets any darker."

Ty opened the gate to the forest and closed it behind them. They rode to the rocky ledge above. Ahead several vultures were gathered around a small body. A closer look revealed that Nirvana was the dead body. Her relaxed mouth and eyes were open and she was awful to look upon. Patti began to cry. Ty dismounted and handing the reins to Patti, walked to a scrap of paper that had fallen from her hand.

"He read, 'I did everything the Secret Organization asked me to do including injecting Sonny Calhoun's cigarettes with the poison they left in my pay envelope. They didn't let me know poison was in that syringe.

Their note lied when it said he would feel better. The note told me where to find his pickup with the door unlocked and pack of cigarettes inside. Patti talked about Sonny's death. I came here to try to find peace. I never intended to cause his death and don't know why my employer wanted him dead." Ty saw blood from a rifle shot wound. Nirvana had bled to death alone in the forest. The shot was from a 30-06 hunting rifle that wasn't at the scene. It was never discovered whether the bullet came accidentally from a hunter's rifle or if The Secret Organization had decided to be rid of Nirvana as they had of Sonny Calhoun. If they no longer wanted her, couldn't they fired her as they did Rodney? Why did a thirteen year old girl have to die?

-The End –

GLOSSARY

Angus - a beef breed of cattle which are either all black or all red.

Apiary - place honeybee hives are placed

Beef Breed-cattle used for meat instead of milk

Border Collie - a breed of dog which likes handling cattle and does this well if well-trained

Bovine - cattle or oxen

Broken mouth cow - a cow that has lost part of her teeth

Charlois - a beef breed of cattle, which are all white or light, yellow

Chokecherry-small sour cherry that grows on bushes beside water such as river or ditch and makes tasty syrup, but doesn't gel when juice is mixed with pectin

Cow-adult female bovine

Cowy-a horse who likes handling cattle

Cow dog-a dog trained to handle cattle

Cow-horse- a well-trained horse used to handle cattle

Dairy breed-cattle used for milk more than meat

Draft horse - Large usually easily gentled horse about 17 to 18 hands tall, heavy bodied, strong, usually used in teams of two, four, or six to pull heavy loads; also called workhorse

Fill - weight put on livestock for sale at auction by letting them eat or drink too much - This causes them to sell for less money

Gelbvieh-a well-mannered beef breed of cattle which are all red.

Gooseberries - a transparent light green sour berry that grows on bushes among rocks

Hampshire - a breed of sheep

Heifer - cow that is one or two years old

Hereford - a beef breed of cattle which are red with a white face and white markings on the neck, brisket, and legs, sometimes with a narrow white line along part of the backbone. Although these cattle are easy to handle, white faces aren't popular now because eyes surrounded by white reflect more light, thus more frequently having cancer eye. Prevention is why black marks are applied under the eyes of football players and white face cattle. The breed originated in Herefordshire, England.

Holstein - a breed of dairy cattle which are black and white or red and white, producing milk with 3% to 4% butterfat, less than milk from a Jersey cow

Hunter-Jumper - tall 16 to 18 hand narrow bodied horse used for jumping or fox hunting

Limousine - a beef breed of cattle either all black or all red

Open cow - cow that isn't pregnant

Quarter-horse - a breed of horse originating in the United States used as cow-horse or race horse

Service berry - (pronounced sarvis)-a dark blue berry which grows wild on a white flowering bush, usually among sagebrush at about 7000 to 9000 feet elevation. The berries are bigger in a wet year and few to none in a dry year

Pinzgauer - a beef breed of cattle which is red with white along the backbone from the middle back through the tail-head

Jersey - a breed of red dairy cattle with large eyes and high cream content milk

Red Devon - a breed of cattle with beef and dairy strains

Saler- a beef breed of cattle

Scotch Highlander - a small hardy beef breed of cattle frequently found in high altitude land.

Service berries - pronounced sarvis, a dark blue berry that grows on mountain bushes among sagebrush

Sheep dog - a dog trained to handle sheep

Shepherd - Sheep protector whom sheep follow as differentiated from person hired to tend and drive sheep

Smooth mouth cow - a cow that doesn't have teeth

Suffolk- a breed of sheep

Thoroughbred horse - a breed of horse used for racing or jumping or hunting which is usually cowy

ACKNOWLEDGEMENTS

Nina Wood - photography of front cover and several other pictures

Mary Clark - publishing and marketing

Sylvia Burleigh - professional editing

Don Off-husband who let me write this book

Richard S. Rose M. A. -professional review

GOD'S WORD

KJV, as are all Bible quotations in this book

Psalm 119:165 "Great peace have they that love Thy law and nothing shall offend them."

Isaiah 26:3 "Thou wilt keep him in perfect peace, whose mind is stayed on Thee, because he trusteth in Thee.

Psalm 119:11 "Thy word have I hid in my heart that 1 might not sin against Thee."

Psalm 119:9 "Where-with-all shall a young man cleanse his way? By taking heed thereto according to Thy word."

Romans 3:10 As it is written, there is none righteous, no not one."

Romans 3:23 "For all have sinned and come short of the glory of God."

Romans 5:8 "But God commendeth His love toward us, in that while we were yet sinners,Christ died for us."

Romans 5:12 "Wherefore, as by one man sin entered the world, and death by sin; and so death passed upon all men,for that all have sinned:"

Romans 6:23 "The wages of sin is death, but the gift of God is eternal life through Jesus Christ our Lord."

Romans 10:13 "For whosoever shall call upon the name of the Lord shall be saved."

Romans 10:9-10 "That if thou shalt confess with thy mouth the Lord Jesus, and shalt believe in thine heart that God hath raised Him from the dead, thou shalt be saved."

Acts 16:31 "Believe on the Lord Jesus Christ and thou shalt be saved."

John 14:6 "Jesus saith unto him, I AM the way, the truth, and the life: no man cometh unto the Father, but by Me."

Ephesians 2:8-10 "For by grace are ye saved through faith, and that not of yourselves: it is the gift of God:not of works, lest any man should boast. For we are His workmanship, created unto good works which God hath before ordained that we should walk in them."

Romans 11:6a "And if by grace, then is it no more of works:"

John 1:12 "But as many as received Him, to them gave He the power to become the sons of God."

John 1:1-4 "In the beginning was the Word,and the Word was with God, and the Word was God.The same was in the beginning with God. All things were made by Him; and without Him was not anything made which was made. In Him was life; and the life was the light of men."

John 1:14 "And the Word was made flesh, and dwelt among us, (and we beheld His glory, the glory as of the only begotten of the Father,) full of grace and truth."

Isaiah 7:14 "Therefore the Lord Himself shall give you a sign; behold a virgin shall conceive, and bear a son, and shall call His name Immanuel."

Colossians 1:16 "For by Him were all things created, that are in heaven, and that are in earth,visible and invisible, whether they be thrones,or dominions, or principalities, or powers: all things were created by Him and for Him."

John 3:3 "Jesus answered and said unto him, Verily, verily I say unto thee, except a man be born again,he cannot see the kingdom of God."I Peter 1:23 "Being born again, not of corruptible seed, but of incorruptible, by the Word of God, which liveth and abideth forever."

John 3:13-18 "And no man hath ascended up to heaven, but He that came down from heaven ,even the Son of man which is in heaven, and as Moses lifted up the serpent in the wilderness, even so must the Son of man be lifted up; that whosoever believeth in Him should not perish, but have eternal life, for God so loved the world, that He gave His only begotten Son, that whosoever believeth in Him should not perish, but have everlasting life. For God sent not His Son into the world to condemn the world; but that the world through Him might be saved. He that believeth in Him is not condemned; but he that believeth not is condemned already, because he hath not believed in the name of the only begotten Son of God."

Acts 4:12 "Neither is there salvation in any other; for there is none other name under heaven given among men,whereby we must be saved."

Numbers 21:9 "And Moses made a serpent of brass, and put it on a pole, and it came to pass, that if a serpent had bitten any man, when he beheld the serpent of brass, he lived."

II Kings 18:4 "He [Hezekiah] removed the high places, and brake the images, and brake in pieces the brazen serpent that Moses had made: for unto those days the children of Israel did burn incense to it: and he called it Nehushtan."

Isaiah 45:21-22 "Tell ye, and bring them near; yea, let them take counsel together: who hath declared this from ancient time? Who hath told it from that time? Have not I the LORD? And there is no God beside Me; a just God and a Savior; there is none beside Me. Look unto Me, and be ye saved, all the ends of the earth:for I AM God, and there is none else."

Hebrews 12:2 "Looking unto Jesus the author and finisher of our faith; Who for the joy that was set before Him endured the cross,despising the shame, and is set down at the right hand of the throne of God."

Deuteronomy 6:4-5 "Hear,O Israel:The LORD our God is one [one here is a plural word like family is plural; plurality in unity; triunity] LORD:

And thou shalt love the LORD thy God with all thine heart, and with all thine soul, and with all thy might."

Titus 3:4-7 "But after the kindness and love of God our Savior toward man appeared, not by works of righteousness which we have done, but according to His mercy He saved us, by the washing of regeneration, and the renewing of the Holy Ghost; which was shed on us abundantly through Jesus Christ our Savior; that being justified by His grace, we would be made heirs according to the hope [hope here means certainty.] of eternal life."

II Peter 3:18 "But grow in grace, and in the knowledge of our Lord and Savior Jesus Christ. To Him be glory both now and forever. Amen."

Hebrews 11:6 "But without faith it is impossible to please God; for he that cometh to God must believe that He is, and that He is a rewarder of them that seek Him."

Habakkuk 2:4 "Behold his soul which is lifted up [proud] is not upright in him: but the just shall live by his faith."

Romans 1:17 "For therein is the righteousness of God revealed from faith to faith: as it is written, the just shall live by faith."

Galatians 3:11 "But that no man is justified by the law in the sight of God, it is evident: for the just shall live by faith."

Hebrews 10:38 "Now the just shall live by faith: but if any man draw back, My soul shall have no pleasure in him."

Hebrews 4:16 "Let us therefore come boldly unto the throne of grace, that we might obtain mercy, and find grace to help in time of need."

Hebrews 10:25 "Not forsaking the assembling of ourselves together, as the manner of some is; but exhorting one another; and so much the more, as ye see the day approaching."

I Thessalonians 4:16-17 "For the Lord Himself shall descend from heaven with a shout, and with the voice of the archangel, and the trump of God: and the dead in Christ shall rise first: then we which are alive and remain shall be caught up together with them in the clouds, to meet the Lord in the air, and so shall we ever be with the Lord."

Philippians 4:4-8 "Rejoice in the Lord always: and again I say rejoice. Let your moderation be known unto all with all thine soul, and with all thy might."

Titus 3:4-7 "But after the kindness and love of God our Savior toward man appeared, not by works of righteousness which we have done, but according to His mercy He saved us, by the washing of regeneration, and the renewing of the Holy Ghost; which was shed on us abundantly through Jesus Christ our Savior; that being justified by His grace, we would be made heirs according to the hope   [hope here means certainty.] of eternal life."

II Peter 3:18 "But grow in grace, and in the knowledge of our Lord and Savior Jesus Christ. To Him be glory both now and forever. Amen."

Hebrews 11:6 "But without faith it is impossible to please God; for he that cometh to God must believe that He is, and that He is a rewarder of them that seek Him."

Habakkuk 2:4 "Behold his soul which is lifted up [proud] is not upright in him: but the just shall live by his faith."

Romans 1:17 "For therein is the righteousness of God revealed from faith to faith: as it is written, the just shall live by faith."

Galatians 3:11 "But that no man is justified by the law in the sight of God, it is evident: for the just shall live by faith."

Hebrews 10:38 "Now the just shall live by faith: but if any man draw back, My soul shall have no pleasure in him."

Hebrews 4:16 "Let us therefore come boldly unto the throne of grace, that we might obtain mercy, and find grace to help in time of need."

Hebrews 10:25 "Not forsaking the assembling of ourselves together, as the manner of some is; but exhorting one another; and so much the more, as ye see the day approaching."

I Thessalonians 4:16-17 "For the Lord Himself shall descend from heaven with a shout, and with the voice of the archangel, and the trump of God: and the dead in Christ shall rise first: then we which are alive and remain shall be caught up together with them in the clouds, to meet the Lord in the air, and so shall we ever be with the Lord."

Philippians 4:4-8 "Rejoice in the Lord always: and again I say rejoice. Let your moderation be known unto all men. The Lord is a hand. Be careful for nothing (don't worry]; but in everything by prayer and supplication with thanksgiving let your requests be made known unto God. And the peace of God which passeth all understanding, shall keep your hearts and minds through Christ Jesus. Finally, brethren, whatsoever things are true, whatsoever things are honest, whatsoever things are just, whatsoever things are pure, whatsoever things are lovely, whatsoever things are of good report, if There be any virtue, if there be any praise, think on these things."

John 14:1-3 "Let not your heart be troubled; ye believe in God, believe also in Me. In My Father's house are many mansions: if it were not so, I would have told you. I go to prepare a place for you. And if I go and prepare a place for you, I will come again and receive you unto Myself, that where I AM, there may ye be also."

Revelation 3:20 "Behold, I stand at the door, and knock; if any man hear my voice, and open the door, I will come into him, and will sup with him, and he with Me."

Isaiah 52:13-14 Behold, My Servant will deal prudently, He shall be exalted and extolled, and be very high. As many as were astonished at Thee; His visage was so marred more than any man, and His form more than the sons of men:

Isaiah 53:1-12 "Who hath believed our report? And to whom is the arm of the LORD revealed? For He shall grow up before him as a tender plant, and as a root out of a dry ground: He hath no form nor comeliness; and when we shall see Him, there is no beauty that we should desire Him, He is despised and rejected of men; a man of sorrows: yet we esteemed Him not. Surely He hath borne our grief's, and carried our sorrows: yet we esteemed Him stricken, smitten of God, and afflicted. But He was wounded for our transgressions, He was bruised for our iniquities: the chastisement of our peace was upon Him; and with His stripes we are healed. All we like sheep are gone astray; we have turned everyone to his own way; and the LORD hath laid on Him the iniquity of us all. He was oppressed and He was afflicted, yet He opened not His mouth. He was taken from prison and from judgment: who shall declare His generation? For He was cut off out of the land of the living; for the transgression of My people was He stricken. And He made His grave with the wicked, and with the rich in His death; because He had done no violence, neither was any deceit in His mouth. Yet it pleased the LORD to bruise Him; He hath put Him to grief: when Thou shalt make His soul an offering for sin, He shall see His seed, He shall prolong His days, and the pleasure of the LORD shall prosper in His hand. He shall see the travail of His soul, and shall be satisfied: by His knowledge shall My righteous Servant justify many; for He shall bear their iniquities. Therefore will I divide Him a portion with the great, and He shall divide the spoil with the strong; because He hath poured out His soul unto death: and He was numbered with the transgressors, and He bare the sin of many, and made intercession for the transgressors."

Isaiah 50:6 "I gave My back to the smiters and My cheeks to them that plucked off the hair: I hid not My face from shame and spitting."

Revelation 1:5 "And from Jesus Christ, Who is the faithful witness, and the first begotten from the dead, and the prince of kings of the earth. Unto Him that loved us, and washed us from our sins with His own blood."

Joshua 1:8 "This book of the law shall not depart out of thy mouth; but thou shalt meditate therin day and night, that thou mayest observe to do according to all that is written therin: for then thou shalt make thy way prosperous, and then thou shalt have good success."

Joshua 24:24-25 "Now therefore, fear the LORD, and serve Him in sincerity and truth: and put away the gods which your fathers served on the other side of the flood, and in Egypt; and serve the LORD. And if it seem evil to you to serve the LORD, choose ye this day whom ye will serve; whether the gods which your fathers served that were on the other side of the flood, or the gods of the Amorites, in whose land ye dwell: but as for me and my house, we will serve the LORD."

Deuteronomy 6:4-5 "Hear,O Israel:the LORD our God is one LORD:and thou shalt love the LORD thy God with all thine heart; and with all thy soul, and with all thy might." [Here one is plural in the sense that family is plural.]

Exodus 21:22-23 "If a man strive, and hurt a woman with child, so that her fruit depart from her, yet no mischief follow: he shall surely be punished, according as the woman's husband will lay on him; and he shall pay as the judges determine. And if any mischief follow, then thou shalt give life for life.""

James 2:10 "For whosoever shall keep the whole law, yet offend in one point, he is guilty of all."

II Chronicles 7:14 "If My people which are called by My name, shall humble themselves, and pray, and seek My face, and turn from their wicked ways; then l will hear from heaven, and will forgive their sin, and will heal their land."

Romans 11:7a "Israel hath not obtained that which he seeketh for; but the election hath obtained it,"

Ephesians 1:4 "According as He hath chosen us [Israelites; Jews] in Him before the foundation of the world, that we should be holy and without blame before Him in love;"

Romans 3:1-4 "What advantage then hath the Jew? Much in every way: chiefly, because that to them were committed the oracles of God. For what if some did not believe? Shall their unbelief make the faith of God without effect? God forbid: yea let God be true, but every man a liar; as it is written, That thou mightest overcome when thou art judged."

Romans 11:11 "I say then, have they stumbled that they should fall? God forbid: but rather through their fall salvation is come unto the Gentiles, for to provoke them to jealousy."

Romans 11:25-26 "For I would not, brethren, that ye should be ignorant of this mystery, lest ye should be wise in your own conceits; that blindness in part is happened to Israel, until the fullness of the Gentiles be come in. And so all Israel shall be saved: as it is written, There shall come out of Sion the Deliverer, and shall turn away ungodliness from Jacob:"

Romans 11:28 "As concerning the gospel, they are enemies for your sakes: but as touching the election, they are beloved for the fathers' sakes."

I John 1:7-9 "But if we walk in the light, as He is in the light, we have fellowship with one another, and the blood of Jesus Christ His Son cleanseth us from all sin. If we say that we have no sin, we deceive ourselves, and the truth is not in us. If we confess our sins, He is faithful and just to forgive us our sins, and to cleanse us from all unrighteousness."

I John 5:11-13 "And this is the record, that God hath given to us eternal life, and this life is in His Son. He that hath the Son hath life; and he that hath not the Son of God hath not life. These things have I written to you that believe on the name of the Son of God; that ye may believe on the name of the Son of God.

Romans 12:1-5 "I beseech you therefore, brethren, by the mercies of God, that ye present your bodies a living sacrifice, holy, acceptable unto God, which is your reasonable service. And be not conformed to this world: but be ye transformed by the renewing of your mind, that ye may prove what is that good, and acceptable, and perfect, will of God. For I say, through the grace given unto me, to every man that is among you, not to think of himself more highly than he ought to think; but to think soberly, according as God hath dealt to every man the measure of faith. For as we have many members in one body, and all members have not the same office: So we, being many, are one body in Christ, and every one members one of another." | Samuel 15:22-23b "Hath the LORD as great delight in burnt offerings and sacrifices, as in obeying the voice of the LORD? Behold to obey is better than sacrifice, and to hearken than the fat of rams. For rebellion is as the sin of witchcraft, and stubbornness is as iniquity and idolatry."

Romans 13:1 "Let every soul be subject unto the higher powers. For there is no power but of God: the powers that be are ordained of God.

Romans 13:10 "Love worketh no ill to his neighbor: therefore love is the fulfilling of the law."

Proverbs 1:10 "My son, if sinners entice thee, consent thou not."

Romans 13:14 "But put ye on the Lord Jesus Christ, and make not provision for the flesh, to fulfil the lusts thereof."

Proverbs 15:3 "The eyes of the LORD are in every place beholding the evil and the good."

Psalm 12:6-7 "The words of the LOED are pure words, as silver tried in a furnace of earth, purified seven times, Thou wilt keep them, O LORD, Thou wilt preserve them."

Psalm 14:1 "The fool hath said in his heart, there is no God. They are corrupt, they have done abominable works, there is none that doeth good,"

Proverbs 3:5 "Trust in the LORD with all thine heart; and lean not unto thine own understanding."

Proverbs 3:6 "In all thy ways acknowledge Him, and He shall direct thy paths."

Proverbs 6:32 "But whoso committeth adultery with a woman lacketh understanding: he that doeth it destroyeth his own soul."

Proverbs 9:10 "The fear of the LORD is the beginning of wisdom: and knowledge of the holy is understanding."

Proverbs 11:30 "The fruit of the righteous is a tree of life; and he that winneth souls is wise."

Daniel 12:3 "And they that be wise shall shine as the brightness of the firmament; and they that turn many to righteousness as the stars forever and ever."

Proverbs 15:1 "A soft answer turneth away wrath: but grievous words stir up anger."

Romans 12:18 "If it be possible, as much as lieth in you, live peaceably with all men."

Proverbs 16:18 "Pride goeth before destruction and a haughty spirit before a fall."

Proverbs 22:1 "A good name is rather to be chosen than great riches, and loving favor rather than silver and gold."

Proverbs 27:1 "Boast not thyself of tomorrow, for thou knowest not what a day may bring forth."

Proverbs 28:13 "He that covereth his sins shall not prosper: but whoso confesseth and forsaketh them shall have mercy."

Matthew 1:1 "The book of the generations of Jesus Christ, the son of David, the son of Abraham."

Genesis 1:1 "In the beginning God created the heaven and the earth."

Colossians 1:16-17 "For by Him were all things created, that are in heaven, and that are in earth, visible and invisible, whether they be thrones, or dominions, or principalities, or powers: all things were created by Him and for Him. And He is before all things and by Him all things consist."

Psalms 8:4-6 "The wicked, through the pride of his countenance, will not seek after God: God is not in all his thoughts."

Psalms 10:4 "The wicked, through the pride of his countenance, will not seek after God: God is not in all his thoughts."

Psalms 20:7 "Some trust in chariots, and some in horses: but we will remember the name of the LORD our God."

Romans 14:10b-12 "...we shall all stand before the judgment seat of Christ. For it is written, As I live, saith the Lord, every knee shall bow to me, and every tongue shall confess to God. So then every one of us shall give account of himself to God."

Romans 14:23b "...whatsoever is not of faith is sin."

Psalms 25:9 "The meek will he guide in judgment: and the meek will He teach His way."

I Samuel 12:23 "Moreover as for me, God forbid that I should sin against the LORD in ceasing to pray for you: but l will teach you the good and right way."

Colossians 1:9 "For this cause we also, since the day we heard it, do not cease to pray for you, and to desire that ye might be filled with the knowledge of His will in all wisdom and spiritual understanding."

Psalms 67:2,4 "That Thy way may be known upon the earth, Thy saving health among all nations, O let the nations be glad and sing for joy: for Thou shalt judge the people righteously, and govern the nations upon the earth. Selah."

Psalm 71:8 "Let thy mouth be filled with Thy praise and with Thy honor all the day."

Psalms 73:24 "Thou shalt guide me with Thy counsel, and afterward receive me to glory."

Psalm 85:6 "Wilt Thou not revive us again: that Thy people may rejoice in Thee?"

Psalm 91:8 "Only with Thine eyes shalt Thou see the reward of the wicked."

Psalm 97:6 "The heavens declare His righteousness, and all the people see His glory."

Revelation 1:7 "Behold, He cometh with clouds; and every eye shall see Him: and all kindreds of the earth shall wail because of Him. Even so, Amen."

Revelation 1:5 "And from Jesus Christ, Who is the faithful witness, and the first begotten from the dead, and the prince of the kings of the earth. Unto Him that loved us, and washed us from our sins in His own blood."

Psalms 98:4 "Make a joyful noise unto the Lord, all the earth: make a loud noise, and rejoice, and sing praise."

Psalms 100:1-5 "Make a joyful noise unto the LORD, all ye lands/ Serve the LORD with gladness; come before His presence with singing. Know ye that the LORD He is God: it is He that hath made us, and not we ourselves; we are His people, and the sheep pasture. Enter into His gates with thanksgiving, and into His courts with praise: be thankful unto Him, and bless His name. For the LORD is good; His mercy is everlasting; and His truth endureth to all generations."

Psalms 105:9-11 "Which covenant He made with Abraham, and His oath to Isaac; and confirmed the same unto Jacob for a law, and to Israel for an everlasting covenant: saying, unto thee will I give the land of Canaan, the lot of your inheritance:"

Genesis 12:1-3: Now the LORD said unto Abram, Get thee out of thy country, and from thy kindred, and from thy father's house, unto a land that I will shew thee: and l will make of thee a great nation, and l Bwill bless thee, and make thy name great; and thou shalt be a blessing: and I will bless them that bless thee, and curse them that curse thee: and in thee shall all the families of the earth be blessed."

Psalm 107:17,19 "Fools because of their transgression, and because of their iniquities, are afflicted ...Then they cry unto the LORD in their trouble, and He saveth them out of their distress."

Ecclesiastes 12:13,14 Let us hear the conclusion of the whole matter: Fear God and keep His commandments: for this is the whole duty of man. For God shall bring every work into judgement, with every secret thing, whether it be good, or whether it be evil."

126

Revelation 3:20 "Behold, I stand at the door and knock: if any man hear My voice, and open the door, I will come in to him, and will sup with him, and he with Me."

Proverbs 14:12 "There is a way which seemeth right to a man, but the end thereof are the ways of death."

Proverbs 19:5 "A false witness shall not be unpunished, and he that speaketh lies shall not escape."

Proverbs 20:11 "Even a child is known by his doings, whether his work be pure, and whether it be pure, and whether it be right."

Proverbs 21:9 "It is better to dwell in the corner of a housetop, than with a brawling woman in a wide house."

Proverbs 21:19 "It is better to dwell in the wilderness, than with a contentious and an angry woman."

Proverbs 21:13 "Whoso stoppeth his ears at the cry of the poor, he also shall cry himself, but shall not be heard."

Proverbs 22:2 " The rich and the poor meet together: the LORD is the Maker of them all."

Proverbs 21:21 "He that followeth after righteousness and mercy findeth life, righteousness, and honour."

Proverbs 21:23 "Whoso keepeth his mouth and his tongue keepeth his soul from troubles."

James 3:6 "And the tongue is a fire, a world of iniquity: so is the tongue among our members, that it defileth the whole body, and setteth on fire the course of nature, and it is set on fire of hell."

Proverbs 22:6 "Train up a child in the way he should go: and when he is old, he will not depart from it." [Here old means the age of hair on the chin. (adolescence)]

Foolishness is bound in the heart of a child; but the rod of correction shall drive it far from him." [Rod = A willow or tamarisk branch stings, but does not injure the buttocks. A hand, belt or razor strap should not spank because those can injure. Discipline should always be with instruction.]

Proverbs 29:15 "The rod and reproof give wisdom: but a child left to himself bringeth his mother to shame."

Proverbs 29:17 "Correct thy son, and he shall give thee rest; yea he shall give delight to thy soul."

Proverbs 29:23-32 "Who hath woe? Who hath sorrow? Who hath contentions? Who hath babbling? Who hath wounds without cause? Who hath redness of eyes? They that tarry long at the wine; they that go to seek mixed wine. Look not at the wine when it is red, when it giveth his colour in the cup, when it moveth itself aright. At the last it biteth like s serpent, and stingeth like an adder. [Are snake bites in moderation okay?]

Proverbs 20:1 "Wine is a mocker and strong drink is raging, whoso is deceived thereby is not wise."

Proverbs 31:6 "Give strong drink unto him that is ready to perish, and wine to those who be of heavy hearts."

Proverbs 24:21 "My son,fear thou the LORD and the king: and meddle not with them that are given to change:"

Proverbs 24:29 "Say not, I will do so to him as he hath done to me: I will render to the man according to his work."

Romans 12:19 "Dearly beloved, avenge not yourselves, but rather give place unto wrath: for it is written, vengeance is Mine; I will repay, saith the Lord."

Deuteronomy 32:35a "To Me belongeth vengeance,and recompense..."

Proverbs 29:23 " A man's pride shall bring him low: but honour shall uphold the humble in spirit."

Romans 15:4 "For whatsoever things were written aforetime were written for our learning, that we through patience and comfort of the scriptures might have hope."

Micah 5:2 "But thou, Bethlehem Ephratah, though thou be little among the thousands of Judah, yet out of thee shall He come forth unto me that is to be ruler in Israel; whose goings forth have been from old, from everlasting."

Matthew 2:1 "Now when Jesus was born in Bethlehem of Judaea in the days of Herod the king, behold there came wise men from the east to Jerusalem,"

Isaiah 53:8 "He was taken from prison and from judgement: and who shall declare His generation? For He was cut off out of the land of the living: for the transgression of My people was He stricken."

Luke 23:46 "And when Jesus had cried with a loud voice, He said, Father, into Thy hands I commend My spirit: and having said thus, He gave up the ghost."

Psalm 16:10 "For Thou wilt not leave My soul in hell; neither wilt Thou suffer Thine Holy One to see corruption."

Acts 2:29-32 "Men and brethren, let me freely speak unto you of the patriarch David, that he is both dead and buried, and his sepulchre is with us this day, therefore being a prophet, and knowing that God had sworn with an oath to him, that of the fruit of his loins, according to the flesh, He would raise up Christ to sit on his throne; He seeing this before spake of the resurrection of Christ, that His soul was not left in hell, neither His flesh did see corruption. This Jesus hath God raised up,where of we are all witnesses."

Lamentations 3:22-23 "It is of the LORD's mercies that we are not consumed, because His compassions" fail not. They are new every morning: great is Thy faithfulness."

I Corinthians 1:18 "For the preaching of the cross is to them that perish foolishness; but unto us which are saved it is the power of God."

I Corinthians 2:5 "That your faith should not stand in the wisdom of men, but in the power of God."

I Corinthians 2:9 "But as it is written, Eye hath not seen, nor ear heard, neither have entered into the heart of man,the things which God hath prepared for them that love him."

I Corinthians 2:14 "But the natural man receiveth not the things of the Spirit of God: for they are foolishness unto him: neither can he know them, because they are spiritually discerned."

I Corinthians 3:13-17 "Every man's work shall be made manifest: for the day shall.declare it, because it shall be revealed by fire; and the fire shall try every man's work of what sort it is. If any man's work abide which he hath built thereupon, he shall receive a reward. If any man's work shall be burned, he shall suffer loss: but he himself shall be saved; yet so as by fire. Know ye not that ye are the temple of God, and that the Spirit of God dwelleth in you? If any man defile the temple of God, him shall God destroy; for the temple of God is holy, which temple ye are."

I Corinthians 3:21a "Therefore let no man glory in men."

I Corinthians 5:11 "But now I have written unto you not to keep company, if any man that is called a brother be a fornicator,or covetous, or an idolater, or a railer, or a drunkard, or an extortioner; with such an one no not to eat."

I Corinthians 5:7b "...Christ our Passover is sacrificed for us.. ."

I Corinthians 5:12,13 "For what have I to do to judge them also that are without? Do not ye judge them that are within? But them that are without God judgeth. Therefore put away from among yourselves that wicked person."

I Corinthians 15:1-4 "Moreover, brethren, I declare unto you the gospel which I preached unto you, which also ye have received, and wherein ye stand; By which also ye are saved, if ye keep in memory what I preached unto you, unless ye have believed in vain. For I delivered

130

unto you first of all that which I also received, how that Christ died for our sins ac- cording to the scriptures; And that he was buried, and that he rose again the third day according to the scriptures:"

I Corinthians 6:1-3 "Dare any of you, having a matter against another, go to law before the unjust, and not before the saints? Do ye not know that the saints shall judge the world? and if the world shall be judged by you, are ye unworthy to judge the smallest matters? Know ye not that we shall judge angels? How much more things that pertain to this life? If then ye have judgments of things pertaining to this life,set them to judge who are least esteemed in the church."

I Corinthians 6:7 "Now therefore there is utterly a fault among you, because ye go to law one with another. Why do ye not rather take wrong? Why do ye not rather suffer yourselves to be defrauded?"

I Corinthians 7:2 "Nevertheless, to avoid fornication, let every man have his own wife, and let every woman have her own husband."

I Corinthians 8:3 "But if any man love God, the same is known of him."

I Corinthians 10:4b "that Rock was Christ."

I Corinthians 10:6 "Now these things were our examples, to the intent we should not lust after evil things, as they also lusted."

I Corinthians 10:13 "There hath no temptation taken you but such as is common to man: but God is faithful, who will not suffer you to be tempted above that ye are able; but will with the temptation also make a way to escape, that ye may be able to bear it."

I Corinthians 10:31b "do all to the glory of God."

I Corinthians 11:3 "But I would have you know, that the head of every man is Christ; and the head of the woman is the man; and the head of Christ is God."

I Corinthians 11:9 "Neither was the man created for the woman; but the woman for the man."

I Corinthians 11:15 "But if a woman have long hair, it is a glory to her: for her hair is given her for a covering."

I Corinthians 11:28 "But let a man examine himself, and so let him eat of that bread, and drink of that cup."

I Corinthians 12:25-27 "That there should be no schism in the body; but that the members should have the same care one for another. And whether one member suffer, all the members suffer with it; or one member be honoured, all the members rejoice with it. Now ye are the body of Christ, and members in particular."

I Corinthians 13:1-13 "Though I speak with the tongues of men and of angels, and have not charity, I am become as sounding brass, or a tinkling cymbal. And though I have the gift of prophecy, and underStand all mysteries,and all knowledge; and though I have all faith, so that I could remove mountains, and have not charity, I am nothing. And though I bestow all my goods to feed the poor, and though I give my body to be burned, and have not charity, it profiteth me nothing. Charity suffereth long, and is kind; charity envieth not; charity vaunteth not itself, is not puffed up, doth not behave itself unseemly, seeketh not her own, is not easily provoked, thinketh no evil; Rejoiceth not in iniquity, but rejoiceth in the truth; beareth all things, believeth all things, hopeth all things, endureth all things. Charity never faileth: but whether there be prophecies,they shall fail; whether there be tongues, they shall cease; whether there be knowledge, it shall vanish away. For we know in part, and we prophesy in part. But when that which is perfect is come, then that which is in part shall be done away. When I was a child, I spake as a child, I understood as a child, I thought as a child: but when I became a man, 1 put away childish things. For now we see through a glass, darkly; but then face to face: now 1 know in part; but then shall 1 know even as also I am known. And now abideth faith, hope, charity, these three; but the greatest of these is charity."

I Corinthians 14:33 "For God is not the author of confusion, but of peace, as in all churches of the saints."

Il Corinthians 1:4 "Who comforteth us in all our tribulation, that we may be able to comfort them which are in any trouble, by the comfort wherewith we ourselves are comforted of God."

II Corinthians 1:9b "...we should not trust in ourselves, but in God which raiseth the dead"

Il Corinthians 1:22 "Who hath also sealed us, and given the earnest of the Spirit in our hearts."

Titus 2:11 "For the grace of God that bringeth salvation hath appeared to all men."

II Chronicles 16a:9 "For the eyes of the LORD run to and fro throughout the whole earth, to shew himself strong in the behalf of them whose heart is perfect toward him."

I Corinthians 7:23 "Ye are bought with a price; be not ye the servants of men."

I Corinthians 7:8-9 "I say therefore to the unmarried and widows, It is good for them if they abide even as I. But if they cannot contain, let them marry: for it is better to marry than to burn.

Isaiah 42:1 "Behold My Servant Whom I uphold: mine elect, in Whom My soul delighteth; I have put My Spirit upon Him: He shall bring forth judgement to the Gentiles."

II Chronicles 30:7 "And be not ye like your fathers, and like your brethren, which trespassed against the LORD God of their fathers, who therefore gave them up to desolation, as ye see."

II Chronicles 30:9b "the LORD your God is gracious and merciful"

II Chronicles 32:8a "With him is an arm of flesh; but with us is the LORD our God to help us, and to fight our battles."

I Corinthians 10:11 "Now all these things happened unto them for examples: and they are written for our admonition, upon whom the ends of the world are come."

I Corinthians 10:7 "Neither be ye idolaters, as were some of them; as it is written, The people sat down to eat and drink, and rose up to play."

I Corinthians 10:23 "All things are lawful for me, but all things are not expedient: all things are lawful for me, but all things edify not."

I Corinthians 10:31 "Whether therefore ye eat,or drink, or whatsoever ye do, do all to the glory of God."

I Corinthians 10:33 "Even as I please all men in all things, not seeking mine own profit, but the profit of many, that they may be saved."

II Timothy 1:12 "For the which cause | also suffer these things: nevertheless 1 am not ashamed: for I know Whom I have believed, and am persuaded that He is able to keep that which I have committed unto Him against that day."

I Corinthians 11:9 "Neither was the man created for the woman; but the woman for the man."

I Corinthians 11:15 "But if a woman have long hair, it is a glory to her: for her hair is given her for a covering."

I Corinthians 11:18b "there be divisions among you"

I Corinthians 11:19a "For there must be also heresies among you,"

I Corinthians 11:23-29 "For I have received of the Lord that which also I delivered unto you, That the Lord Jesus the same night in which he was betrayed took bread: And when he had given thanks, he brake it, and said, Take, eat: this is my body, which is broken for you: this do in remembrance of me. After the same manner also he took the cup, when he had supped, saying, This cup is the new testament in my blood: this do ye, as oft as ye drink it, in remembrance of me. For as often as ye eat this bread, and drink this cup, ye do shew the Lord's death till he come. Wherefore whosoever shall eat this bread, and drink this cup of the Lord, unworthily, shall be guilty of the body and blood of the Lord. But let a man examine himself, and so let him eat of that bread, and drink of that cup. For he that eateth and drinketh unworthily, eateth and drinketh damnation to himself, not discerning the Lord's body."

II Peter 1:16-21 "For we have not followed cunningly devised fables, when we made known unto you the power and coming of our Lord Jesus Christ, but were eyewitnesses of His majesty.For He received from God the Father honour and glory, when there came such a voice to Him from the excellent glory, "This is My beloved Son, in Whom I Am well pleased. And this voice which came from heaven we heard,when we were with Him on the holy mount. We have also a more sure word of prophecy; whereunto ye do well that ye take heed, as unto a light that shineth in a dark place, until the day dawn, and the day star arise in your hearts: Knowing this first, that no prophecy of scripture is of any private interpretation. For the prophecy came not in old time by the will of man: but holy men of God spake as they were moved by the Holy Ghost."

II Timothy3:16 "All scripture is given by inspiration of God, and is profitable for doctrine, for reproof,for correction, for instruction in righteousness."

II Corinthians 6:14 "2Co 6:14 Be ye not unequally yoked together with unbelievers: for what fellowship hath righteousness with unrighteousness? and what communion hath light with darkness?"

Ephesians 5:8-10 "And be not drunk with wine, wherein is excess; but be filled with the Spirit. Speaking to yourselves in psalms and hymns and spiritual songs, singing and making melody in your heart to the Lord;Giving thanks always for all things unto God and the Father in the name of our Lord Jesus Christ."

Proverbs 11:21 Though hand join in hand, the wicked shall not be unpunished: but the seed of the righteous shall be delivered.

Proverbs 16:7 When a man's ways please the LORD, he maketh even his enemies to be at peace with him. Proverbs 30:15-16 The horseleech hath two daughters, crying, Give, give. There are three things that are never satisfied, yea, four things say not, It is enough: The grave; and the barren womb; the earth that is not filled with water; and the fire that saith not, It is enough.

Proverbs 30:33 Surely the churning of milk bringeth forth butter, and the wringing of the nose bringeth forth blood: so the forcing of wrath bringeth forth strife.

Proverbs 31:11-12 The heart of her husband doth safely trust in her, so that he shall have no need of spoil. She will do him good and not evil all the days of her life.

CPSIA information can be obtained
at www.ICGtesting.com
Printed in the USA
BVHW042233290922
PP14087000001B/2